The Glowing Heart

A Josefina Mystery

by Valerie Tripp

★ American Girl®

Special thanks to Judy Woodburn

Published by American Girl Publishing
Copyright © 2016 American Girl

Printed in China
16 17 18 19 20 21 LEO 11 10 9 8 7 6 5 4 3 2 1

All American Girl marks, BeForever™, Josefina™, and Josefina Montoya™
are trademarks of American Girl.

This book is a work of fiction. Any similarity to real persons, living or dead,
is coincidental and not intended by American Girl. References to real events,
people, or places are used fictitiously. Other names, characters, places, and
incidents are the products of imagination.

Lyrics for "Cradle Song" by Sharon Burch from the album *Colors of My Heart*,
courtesy Canyon Records, Phoenix, Arizona. All rights reserved. Lyrics are quoted
on pp. 9–10, 28, 30, 34, 84, and 141.

Cover image by Juliana Kolesova

The following individuals and organizations have given permission to
use images incorporated into the cover design: landscape in lower panel,
© iStock.com/Dean_Fickar; floral element, © iStock.com/Hulinska Yevheniia;
background pattern on back cover, © kirstypargeter/Crestock.

Cataloging-in-Publication Data available from the Library of Congress.

americangirl.com/service

For our family in New Mexico:
Susie, Russell, and Trevor Martin
with love

Beforever™

The adventurous characters you'll meet in
the BeForever books will spark your curiosity
about the past, inspire you to find your voice
in the present, and excite you about your future.
You'll make friends with these girls as you share
their fun and their challenges. Like you, they are
bright and brave, imaginative and energetic,
creative and kind. Just as you are, they are
discovering what really matters: Helping others.
Being a true friend. Protecting the earth.
Standing up for what's right. Read their stories,
explore their worlds, join their adventures.
Your friendship with them will BeForever.

TABLE *of* CONTENTS

1 The Kings' Cake 1

2 Sensible and Serious................15

3 A Flash of Red 27

4 Señor Fernando 39

5 The Ring Is Gone.................64

6 Who Was at the Stream?...........83

7 Lucita...........................108

8 The Wind 130

9 The Truth 144

10 Hearts Aglow 161

   Inside Josefina's World 170

   Glossary of Spanish Words........172

Josefina and her family speak Spanish,
so you'll see some Spanish words in this book.
You'll find the meanings and pronunciations of
these words in the glossary starting on page 172.

Remember that in Spanish, "j" is
pronounced like "h." That means Josefina's
name is pronounced "ho-seh-FEE-nah."

chapter 1

The Kings' Cake

"AH! JOSEFINA, IT'S beautiful!" said Abuelita. "You've done a fine job, dear girl!"

"*Gracias,*" said Josefina, blushing. With quiet pride, she placed the Kings' Cake in front of her grandmother, Abuelita, and then stepped away and clasped her hands behind her back, bowing her head to hide her smile.

Josefina's whole family was gathered in the family *sala*, which looked cozy and festive tonight. All the candles in the hanging chandelier were lit, as well as the candles in the best silver candlesticks. Firelight from the corner hearth warmed the *adobe* walls and gave them a rosy color. It was January sixth, and the Montoyas were celebrating La Fiesta de los Reyes Magos, the Feast of the Three Kings, which marked the day in the Christmas story when the three kings brought their precious gifts of gold, frankincense, and myrrh to the stable where baby Jesus had been born. This year, the Montoya family was celebrating with a Kings' Cake, which Josefina's stepmother, Tía Dolores, had taught her to make.

"A masterpiece," pronounced her grandfather, Abuelito, as Abuelita cut and served thick slices of the rich cake. Abuelito turned to his friend, Don Javier, who was visiting. "I'm sure you've never seen such a fine Kings' Cake even in Mexico City, have you, *amigo*?"

"Never!" said Don Javier. He held his plate above his head as if it were a crown. "It's truly fit for a king—or three kings!" he said, laughing heartily at his own joke.

Everyone else laughed, too, except Josefina's next-oldest sister, Clara, who did not approve of clowning, and her little nephews, Antonio and Juan, who were still impatiently waiting to be served their cake.

They eyed Don Javier's plate with concern, knowing that their mother, Josefina's eldest sister, Ana, would never allow them to play with *their* food in such a way. *And why would they want to?* Josefina thought sympathetically. Cake was meant to be *eaten*, especially this cake, which was the last and best surprise in a day full of surprises. In the morning, the boys had found gifts from the three kings in the shoes they'd left out the night before filled with hay for the kings' camels. If that were not wonderful enough, now they were going to have a *cake* that had a surprise in it! Tía Dolores had introduced the family to the Mexican custom that a token—a bean, a trinket, candy, a whole almond, or a coin—was baked into the Kings' Cake for some lucky person to find in his slice. Finding the token was an omen of great good luck and the promise of a year full of blessings.

Josefina put one arm around Antonio and the other around Juan. The boys were trying as hard as they could to sit still, but they were wiggly with

excitement. Josefina understood; Antonio was only
four, and Juan was only six, and though she and her
sisters Clara and Francisca were much older than
the boys, they were excited, too. In fact, when everyone had been served, Josefina noticed that even the
grown-ups eagerly examined each forkful of cake,
hoping to find the token.

"Oh, oh, *oh!*" crowed Juan. "Look!" He popped
off his seat on the *banco* and held up a shiny coin, his
eyes bright with joy. "I found it! It's mine! The token
was in *my* piece of cake!"

"*Felicidades!*"

"*Muy bien,* Juan!"

"*Excelente!*"

Everyone showered Juan with congratulations,
praising him and fussing over him. Juan bounced
proudly from person to person to show off the coin.
"That's a sign of good fortune, indeed, Juan," said
Abuelito exuberantly as he patted Juan on the back.
"*Bien hecho, mijo*! Well done!"

Josefina saw that poor little Antonio's big brown eyes were full of tears of disappointment as he sat eating his cake. Josefina's heart ached for him. She was a youngest child, too, and she knew how hard it was sometimes. To make Antonio feel better, she said gently, "Antonio, do you want the rest of my cake?"

Antonio nodded and finished Josefina's cake in two bites.

"I think your Tía Dolores would like more cake as well," said Don Javier. "Antonio, little man, I'll ask you to bring this to her, please." He handed Antonio a plate, winking conspiratorially at Josefina over Antonio's head.

Hmm, thought Josefina. *I wasn't the only one who noticed Antonio's tears. Don Javier makes jokes, but he is observant. There is more to him than meets the eye!*

Antonio, good boy that he was, carried the cake to Tía Dolores, who smiled, thanked him, and affectionately brushed his cheek with her hand. But her smile changed to a look of puzzlement when her fork clinked against something hard under her slice of cake. "That's odd," she said. "Antonio, my love, what have you done? Have you hidden something under my cake?" Delicately, Tía Dolores lifted the cake with her fork. She gasped. It was unusual to see Tía Dolores so flustered. Everyone leaned forward to see what had surprised her. They gasped in astonishment, too, when she held up a gorgeous gold-and-ruby ring!

"Oh, ho!" laughed Abuelito. "Don Javier, you always *were* the most devious jokester. I can see you're up to your old tricks! And Antonio, how clever of you to help him! Smart boy!"

Antonio beamed. He was proud and pleased to be just as important and just as praised as his big brother Juan.

Abuelito explained, "The beautiful ring is for you, Dolores. It's your inheritance from your Tía Guadalupe, in gratitude for how well and lovingly you cared for her in Mexico City all those years."

"I remember this ring," said Tía Dolores rather faintly, with a small, sad smile. She held the ring up. The heart-shaped ruby set in the middle of the slender gold band glowed a warm, rich red when the firelight shone through it. "My aunt called this ring the Glowing Heart."

"Ahhh," sighed everyone in admiration.

"*Sí*, the Glowing Heart," said Don Javier. "You left Mexico City before your aunt's will was read, Dolores. When your father heard that I was coming to visit him, he asked me to bring the ring with me and deliver it safely to you, which I've now done for all to see."

"Gracias, Don Javier," said Tía Dolores. "It's a gift I'll treasure. Thank you for bringing it to me."

"You're welcome," said Don Javier. He bowed, and then looked up with a mischievous expression. "And I've brought other gifts, too." With a swiftness that was magical, Don Javier pulled from his sleeve four fluttery silk handkerchiefs—one sky blue, one the purple of the mountains, one corn yellow, and one as orange as the setting sun—which he presented with a flourish to Josefina and her sisters Ana, Francisca, and Clara. As the sisters murmured, "*Muchas gracias*," Don Javier made little wooden carved horses for Juan and Antonio appear—*presto!*—in his hands.

The two boys clapped, awed by the seeming magic. Round-eyed, they whispered their thanks to Don Javier and bowed like little gentlemen as they took their horses. Their mother, Ana, could see that they were itching to play, so with her permission, the boys happily galloped their new toy horses across the hearth, pretending that the horses jumped and reared and made whinnying noises. They raced them along the floor and made them fly past the colorful woven hangings that decorated the walls.

All too soon, a trusted family servant named Teresita appeared in the doorway. When Juan and Antonio visited the *rancho,* Teresita helped Ana by taking care of the boys. "Juan and Antonio," Teresita said, "it's time for bed. *Vamos.*" Both boys were too well mannered and too fond of Teresita to protest. But Antonio's face looked so cloudy and stubborn that he didn't *need* to say anything to make it clear that he was reluctant to leave the party.

"Antonio," his father, Tomás, said in a warning tone. But still Antonio looked mulish.

Lovingly, Teresita scooped him up and began to sing a lullaby. She sang it in Navajo, the language she had spoken as a child:

> *She'awéé' ałts'ísí t'áadoo nichaaí, t'áadoo nichaaí.*
> *Hazhó'ígo íłhosh,*
> *Hazhó'ígo íłhosh k'ad,*
> *Hazhó'ígo íłhosh.*

Josefina and her sisters, seated on the banco by the wall next to the hearth, sang along. They knew the words to the song because Teresita so often sang Juan and Antonio to sleep with it. Teresita had taught them that the words meant:

My baby, little one, do not cry, do not cry.
Softly may you sleep,
Softly may you sleep now,
Softly may you sleep.

Tía Dolores gracefully moved to her piano and picked out the tune, and Papá, much to everyone's delight, played it on his violin. The music filled the room with soft, gentle beauty.

"What a lovely tune that is!" said Don Javier. He hummed along, and then when the song was over, he gave an exaggerated yawn. "My! That lullaby makes me sleepy." He nodded toward Antonio's horse, which Antonio was holding in his hand. "I think your horse is tired, too, my friend," said Don Javier. "He walked all the way from Mexico City to Santa Fe and then to this rancho, and now he wants to rest. You'd better put him to bed, don't you think?"

The grown-ups laughed softly, and Antonio nodded, then nestled his head against Teresita's shoulder.

Teresita held out her free hand to Juan, and off to their sleeping sala the little boys went.

When they had left, Don Javier said to Tía Dolores, "Hearing you play the piano reminds me of musical evenings at your Tía Guadalupe's fine house in Mexico City. Do you remember?"

"Sí," said Tía Dolores. She looked at the ruby ring on her finger. "The ring reminds me, too."

Josefina's sister Francisca gave Josefina a nudge with her elbow and raised her eyebrows as if to say, *My! Isn't the ring beautiful? See how Tía Dolores admires it!*

Josefina thought that Francisca was right: The ring was very beautiful. The ruby in the ring was as red as red peppers, as red as ripe apples, as red as the splendid scarf of the finest wool that Don Javier wore. Clearly, the ring was precious to Tía Dolores, and brought back precious memories of the life she had left behind in Mexico City. Three years ago, Josefina's mamá had died, and Tía Dolores had returned to

New Mexico to help their family on the rancho. Much to Josefina and her sisters' delight, Tía Dolores and Papá had fallen in love and married. The rancho was a happy home again. Thanks to Tía Dolores, it was full of harmony and love.

As if Don Javier had read Josefina's mind, he spoke about Mexico City. "Remember Diablo, that stallion of mine that you used to ride, Dolores?" he said. "What a fine steed! No other woman could control him! Don't you miss him?"

"We have fine horses here, too," said Tía Dolores.

Papá nodded, but Josefina heard the regretful resolve in his voice as he said, "I have to sell Valiente, our finest stallion of all, I'm sorry to say, in order to buy sheep. We are still rebuilding our flocks, trying to replace the sheep we lost a year and a half ago in a flood."

"A flood?" asked Don Javier.

"A terrible, terrible flood!" exclaimed Abuelito.

Josefina shuddered, recalling the flood. Even calm

Papá, who never exaggerated, used vivid words as he described the flood's violence and destruction. "It was a cruel avalanche of water," he said, "sweeping down from the mountains and gushing though the arroyos so fast and furiously that hundreds of sheep were drowned, and crops were lost. The church in the village was badly damaged."

"A disaster!" interjected excitable Abuelito.

"It was Dolores who had the idea of asking Teresita and the girls to weave extra blankets so that we could sell some to buy more sheep," said Papá, looking at his wife, Tía Dolores, proudly. "Thanks to Dolores's idea, the girls' hard work, and Teresita's skill, there is hope that someday our flocks will be as large as they were before the flood. But it's slow and costly to rebuild them."

"I wish you didn't have to sell Valiente," said Tía Dolores sadly.

Papá put his lips together firmly, making it clear that his decision was made.

"Well, *I* wish I could buy Valiente," said Don Javier to Papá. "But I can't, and I sympathize with you." He smiled a sad and sorry smile as he said, "I know how it feels to lose a treasure."

Josefina saw that Don Javier was looking at Tía Dolores, who was twisting the ruby ring on her finger. Josefina wondered: *Was Tía Dolores the treasure he had lost? Or did he mean that he was sorry to part with the ring? Perhaps he had come to think of it as his own on the long, five-month journey from Mexico City, while he was bringing it to Tía Dolores. Or had he lost something valuable of his own in Mexico?* Don Javier was such a flirt and such a joker that it was impossible to tell *what* he meant.

chapter 2

Sensible and Serious

"SOMEDAY *I'M* GOING to have a ring like the Glowing Heart," said Francisca, who was seventeen and very romantic. She looked at her ringless hand and sighed deeply. It was later. The sisters were in their sleeping sala, having said their evening prayers with the family, been blessed by the grown-ups, and then sent to bed.

"*Humph*," snorted practical Clara, who was fourteen. "You'll need a life to go with it, too. It's ridiculous to wear a ring like that while doing chores like ours, on a rancho like ours."

"Think of the wealthy style of life Tía Dolores must have had in Mexico City," said Francisca dreamily as she got into bed. "She gave up a lot when she came here, married Papá, and settled down

15

to life on the rancho. Oh, and did you see the way Don Javier looked at her? I bet Don Javier wanted to marry her, and I bet he's rich, too."

"He does dress elegantly," said Josefina. "That fancy red scarf that he wears is very fine."

"I can't tell if he's rich or not," said Clara tartly. "I can't even tell when he's telling the truth or not. I like people to say what they mean. Don Javier makes me uneasy, because he likes to make silly jokes and trick people. What's the difference between a trick and a lie? It's dishonest to deceive people. I'm not sure that I like Don Javier."

"You liked the silk handkerchief he gave you well enough," said Francisca with a teasing grin.

"And he was nice to Antonio," Josefina added.

"Nice?" asked Clara. "First he hoodwinked Antonio into playing a joke on Tía Dolores, and then he tricked Antonio into thinking that he's a magician who can make little wooden horses appear out of thin air. I call that sneaky and deceptive." Clara pulled her covers up to her chin. "All I'm saying is that I don't trust him," she said. "He's... *slippery*. And he's not sensible or serious."

"Oh, *sensible* and *serious*," groaned Francisca, flapping her hand as if she were dismissing the very ideas as boring.

"What do you think he meant when he said that he'd lost his treasure?" asked Josefina.

"Probably that he has lost his fortune, which he wouldn't have done if he'd been *sensible* and *serious*," said Clara, looking pointedly at Francisca as she emphasized the words. "He's lost his money and that's why he can't buy Papá's horse."

"Oh, Don Javier probably has too many horses already," said Francisca with breezy impatience. "No, no, no, Tía Dolores is the treasure he lost. As I was saying, if Tía Dolores had married Don Javier, she wouldn't have a care in the world! He's so lighthearted!"

"Light-headed," muttered Clara into her pillow.

But Francisca talked over her. "Tía Dolores would've lived the life of a fine lady with him in Mexico City," she said. "There'd be no drudgery for her, no weaving, no working in vegetable gardens as she does here on the rancho. She'd have no endless, boring household chores! In fact, she'd have no chores of *any* sort." Francisca gave Josefina a playful poke. "She wouldn't have to teach *you* to cook, Josefina, which takes the patience of a saint."

"That's true," said Clara. "You do make a lot of mistakes, Josefina. Your *tortillas* are too thick and your *bizcochitos* are too thin."

"Well," Josefina began, "they *taste* all right, and—"

But Francisca talked over Josefina, too. "Tía Dolores wouldn't have all the headache of bookkeeping for the blankets-for-sheep business. No—"

"The business was her idea!" Josefina protested. "I think she likes it."

"Well, *I* wouldn't," said Francisca. "With Don Javier, Tía Dolores wouldn't have all the worries that she and Papá have had ever since the flood, when so many of our sheep were killed."

"Did you hear Papá say that he has to sell his best, most favorite stallion, Valiente, to get money to buy more sheep?" said Clara. "And did you see that Papá and Tía Dolores don't agree about selling Valiente?"

Josefina had to admit it: What Clara said was true. Papá and Tía Dolores did *not* agree about selling Papá's horse. Was Clara also correct when she said that Don Javier wasn't trustworthy? He *was* unpredictable and—what was Clara's word? *Slippery.* Was Francisca correct about the carefree life Tía Dolores could have had if she'd married him? Did Tía Dolores miss the life of wealth and privilege and ease she'd had in Mexico City?

No, thought Josefina. Tía Dolores was always brisk and cheerful, full of energy and ideas and drive! She had made the rancho—and Josefina's heart—alive with music, love, and joy. She loved Josefina and her sisters and Papá as much as they loved her. Tía Dolores had never given the slightest hint that she disliked her demanding life on the rancho, not ever.

And with that confident and comforting thought, Josefina snuggled under her cozy sheepskin covers and went to sleep.

But early the next morning, Josefina's confidence and comfort were sorely shaken.

"No, gracias, Carmen," said Tía Dolores, when the cook offered her a cup of hot chocolate.

That's odd, thought Josefina. Tía Dolores usually relished her morning chocolate. But then, usually Tía Dolores's low and musical voice led the family when they gathered for morning prayers before breakfast, whereas today, Josefina had noticed that Tía Dolores's voice was only a whisper, and she had drooped, leaning against the wall as if for support, her face looking long and pale.

"Tía Dolores hasn't touched her food," Josefina said as the sisters gathered the breakfast plates. She forced herself to ask, "Do you think she's… unwell?"

Josefina's sisters looked at her with concerned faces. She knew they were remembering, as she was, the unhappy time of Mamá's illness. How distressing if Tía Dolores, who was their dearly beloved stepmother now, should become sick.

Francisca was the first to speak up. "Sí, Tía Dolores is sick at heart," she said. "She's terribly, terribly sad about saying good-bye to Abuelito and Abuelita when they leave to return to Santa Fe this morning. Ana, Tomás, and Juan are leaving, too, and I'm sure Tía Dolores dreads sinking back into our usual dull routine, now that the holidays are over. I don't blame her. I dread it, too."

"Don't be so dramatic," chided Clara, clattering the dishes together. "It's natural for Tía Dolores to miss her parents. But I don't think life on the rancho will be dull; after all, Papá and Tía Dolores have asked Antonio to stay for a while."

Josefina smiled. "That's right," she agreed. Life was always lively when Antonio was around! It was great fun to have such a sweet, impish little boy visiting. "And Don Javier is staying, too."

Francisca raised her eyebrows. "I don't think *he* will cure Tía Dolores's heartsickness," she said, sounding wise and superior. "He's the cause of it! He's a reminder of all that she has given up."

Josefina and Clara exchanged exasperated looks. They both found it annoying when Francisca acted as if she understood life, love, romance, and grown-ups better than they did just because she was older than they were!

All the same, Josefina was determined to find out why Tía Dolores wasn't behaving like her usual cheerful self, so she kept a close eye on her during the noise and activity of Abuelito and Abuelita's departure. Papá, Tomás, and Miguel, who was the husband of Carmen, the cook, loaded baskets, sacks, and small trunks onto Abuelito's wagon.

"*Adiós,*" Tía Dolores said as she gave Abuelita a long, hard hug good-bye. "*Vaya con Dios!*"

"You'll be in my prayers every day," said Abuelita, her eyes bright with tears.

"And mine, as well, dear Tía Dolores," said Ana lovingly.

"We'll miss you," said Abuelito, patting Tía Dolores's shoulder. Then he spoke to Abuelita and Ana. "Come along, come along, my dears. We have a long trip ahead."

Ana got into the wagon first, reached down to help Abuelita and Juan, and then settled a warm blanket over their knees. Abuelito sat next to Tomás on the driver's seat. He took the reins, clucked to the horses to walk on, and then waved exuberantly, calling out his good-byes over his shoulder, "Adiós! Muchas gracias!"

As Tía Dolores, Papá, and the sisters waved in

return, the sun caught the ruby of Tía Dolores's ring and made it flash red. The family lingered until they couldn't see the wagon anymore, and then they turned away. Josefina saw Papá smile sympathetically at Tía Dolores before he headed to the fields. Tía Dolores sighed, then straightened her back and squared her shoulders.

Josefina slipped her hand into Tía Dolores's. "You'll miss Abuelito and Abuelita, won't you?" she asked. Josefina knew how it felt to miss someone; she still missed her mother every day even though she loved Tía Dolores, who had shown her that her heart could grow to have room enough for *everyone* she loved.

The wind had loosened a strand of Josefina's hair and as Tía Dolores tucked it behind Josefina's ear, her ring was cold against Josefina's cheek. "Yes," she said. "I'll miss them, especially now."

Josefina looked up with a questioning expression.

"Winter is long," explained Tía Dolores, holding her *rebozo* tight around herself with her free hand.

"And I won't be going to Santa Fe for a quite while." She paused, then said, "Come now, there's work to be done."

"Oh, yes!" said Josefina, swinging hands with Tía Dolores. She was happy, because she'd thought of something that was sure to cheer up Tía Dolores. "Today's the day we visit Santiago and Angelito, isn't it?"

Santiago was a blind shepherd who lived with his grandson Angelito. During the warm months, Santiago and Angelito camped, following Papá's sheep as they grazed through the mountains. Santiago loved the mountains, and stayed as high up on them as possible all year round. In the winter, he and Angelito lived in a hut perched on a mountain just below the snow line. It was the Montoyas' tradition that every year on the day after the Feast of the Three Kings, they brought gifts and food to Santiago and Angelito. Last year, Josefina and Tía Dolores had enjoyed the trip tremendously.

Now, on this bright, brisk January morning, Josefina was sure that a mountain trek was just the thing to blow away Tía Dolores's doldrums. "The gifts and food are packed and ready to go," she said. "Is there anything I can do to help you get ready?"

Tía Dolores squeezed her hand. "I won't be going up the mountain today," she said. "Teresita will go in my place. You and Teresita and Miguel must give my greetings to Santiago and Angelito. Will you do that for me?"

Josefina nodded and smiled, but it was a pretend smile. Actually, she felt worried. Usually, there was nothing Tía Dolores liked better than to be out of doors doing something exhilarating and energetic like taking a long hike up the mountain. What had brought about this sad change? Why had Tía Dolores decided to stay home? With all her heart, Josefina wanted to know.

chapter 3

A Flash of Red

A SHARP AND playful breeze lifted the fringe of Josefina's *sarape* as she and Miguel and Teresita climbed up the steep mountain path. Josefina's spirits lifted, too. Surely she was foolish to worry about Tía Dolores! What could possibly be wrong with *anyone* on such a gloriously sunny day? Josefina looked back over her shoulder. Between the dark green of the pine trees she saw the soft ochre and tan of the foothills and below them, the brown fields and the slender swaths of green on either side of the stream that ran through the rancho. Her heart beat hard not only because she was out of breath from climbing, but also because she felt happy as she looked at the serene rancho below.

"Are you warm enough, Josefina?" asked Teresita. "I'm sure Santiago wouldn't mind if you wore this blanket we're bringing for him. After all," she smiled, "you helped me make it."

Josefina returned the smile fondly as Teresita offered her the blanket. Weaving lessons with Teresita were a great source of pleasure and pride to her. It felt wonderful to Josefina to contribute to the welfare of the family and the rancho. Josefina was grateful to Teresita for teaching her to weave on the upright loom, just as Teresita had learned when she was a little girl. Though the blanket they were bringing to Santiago was new, it looked similar to the old, well-worn blanket Teresita was wearing. Both had red stripes and ended in a fringe.

"No, gracias, I don't need the blanket," said Josefina, her cheeks as red as the fringe. "Walking warms me!" She grinned. "Our blanket will warm Santiago, too. Just think how cozy he'll be at night." She began to sing Teresita's lullaby:

> *She'awéé' ałts'ísí t'áadoo nichaaí, t'áadoo nichaaí.*

"That lullaby worked like magic when you sang it to Antonio last night," Josefina said to Teresita.

"It takes magic to slow Antonio down!" said Teresita. Then she smiled, saying, "Antonio reminds me of my little brother. His name was Níyol, which means Wind. And that was a good name for him, because he was as fast as the wind, and as invisible, too, when he wanted to be. He was always full of energy, like Antonio, and just as stubborn when he didn't want to go to bed!" She laughed. "But the lullaby worked its magic when my mother sang it to Níyol, too, when he was a little boy, just as it worked on Antonio. I'm sure that, wherever he is, Níyol remembers that tune as well as I do."

Josefina was quiet. Teresita seldom spoke about her life before she was a *cautiva*. She was such a beloved and important part of Josefina's family now that Josefina often forgot the terrible sorrow Teresita must have felt—and must still feel—about being taken away from her own family against her will to live among strangers who spoke a different language and had different customs. Josefina thought of Teresita's lullaby. The tune was so beautiful and haunting, and the meaning of the words as Teresita had translated them for her was so gentle and loving. They were the only Navajo words Josefina knew, but their meaning taught her something about how full the life Teresita had known must have been. Like Josefina, Teresita had lost a loving mother—the mother who had sung that lullaby to her. Josefina sang it again, this time more thoughtfully, and Teresita joined in:

> *Hazhó'ígo íłhosh k'ad,*
> *Hazhó'ígo íłhosh.*

"Ah," said Miguel. "Your singing is so sweet it will enchant the forest animals. They'll follow us!"

"I have a feeling that they *are* following us," said Josefina. "I think I've seen a deer appearing and disappearing among the trees and peeking at us shyly. And once in a while, I've seen a bit of red, as if a bird is flitting by above, keeping an eye on us. But the deer and the bird are so swift that I can't ever quite see them clearly. It's nice, though, isn't it, to think that kindly woodland creatures are keeping us company and watching over us?"

"It is," said Teresita. "You do well to catch even glimpses of them. It's those sharp eyes of yours! Next time I go looking for plants to make dyes, you must come with me. You're my best helper at spotting just the right plants to make beautiful colors."

"I'd love to help you!" said Josefina.

Music filled the shepherds' hut:

Happy shepherds,
Goodness has triumphed!
Heaven has opened!
Life has been born!

As Josefina and Angelito sang "The Shepherds' Song," Santiago played the cheerful tune on his flute.

They had started singing after Miguel, Teresita, and Josefina had delivered their gifts and goods to a thankful Santiago and Angelito. In return, the shepherds had served them welcome cups of hot, sweet tea and a spicy stew. Santiago was very pleased with his new blanket, and Teresita was pleased because Santiago had prepared for her a big soft bundle of sheep's wool to bring back to the rancho. She was very grateful to him for doing the time-consuming labor of washing, picking, and carding the wool so that it was ready to be spun, dyed, and woven into blankets.

Teresita insisted on going outside and strapping the bundle onto Miguel's mule immediately, while Josefina and Miguel finished drinking their tea. She was gone for a while, and returned looking wind-blown and happy.

But, as enjoyable as it was to sing along with Santiago's flute, the visitors couldn't linger long at the shepherds' hut. Too soon it was time to begin the trek back down the mountain. So, after finishing their tea, and expressing many thanks for the stew and the bundle of carded wool, the three visitors stood up to leave.

As the shepherds and their guests stepped out of the hut, Josefina could see that already the snow on the mountaintop above was pink from the setting sun. Smoke from the fire in the hut hung low, like a gray cloud, making Josefina's eyes water and casting a filmy dusk.

"Vaya con Dios," said Santiago. He and Angelito stood in the shadow of the hut. "Be safe, and be careful." He hesitated, and then went on soberly. "We've heard rumors of thieves and raiders roaming the mountainside lately. So be alert, and don't tarry. You must not be on the mountain after dark."

Miguel frowned, and Teresita's face creased in concern. Josefina knew that there were often such ominous rumors, and if what Santiago had heard was true, it meant grave danger. Conflict between Spanish landowners like Papá and some of the Apache, Comanche, and Navajo Indians flared up and died down, but always loomed. Each side distrusted the other. When times were bad, they raided settlements and stole horses and other livestock from each other. Sometimes women and children were taken as captives, as Teresita had been. The fighting could be brutal. Josefina shivered, thinking about Santiago's warning.

"We had better hurry along, then," said Miguel, sounding worried. "I will tell Señor Montoya the rumor about thieves and raiders."

Josefina and Teresita said quick good-byes, and headed down the trail behind Miguel and the mule.

After they had walked for a while, Josefina was tired, so she and Teresita rode the mule as Miguel led it. Still, their progress was slow, and Josefina felt stiff with cold. To warm her, Teresita put her arms around her and sang the lullaby:

She'awéé' ałts'ísí t'áadoo nichaaí, t'áadoo nichaaí.

Josefina sighed, sinking into the comfort of
Teresita's embrace. She was so drowsy that she
drifted in and out of sleep. She tried to stay awake
by finding shapes in the rocky outcroppings and
their shadows. One rock looked like a camel's head,
another looked like Noah's Ark, and another looked
like a standing man staring down at them.

Wait! Josefina sat up, suddenly alert, and rubbed
her eyes. Was that a *real* man—wearing a blanket—standing still as a statue? And why did she
see a flash of red? Rocks and shadows had no color!
She had seen the flash of red before, on the way
up the mountain. Then she'd thought it was a bird,
but could it have been a stripe on a man's blanket?
Josefina shuddered, feeling ill at ease and filled
with fear all over again as she thought of Santiago's
warning about thieves and raiders on the mountain.
Maybe the rumor was true. Maybe there were creatures watching them who were *not* kindly. Certainly,
if it was a real man watching them, slithering among

the trees as sly and silent as a snake, it was very serious. The bad men who sneaked down from the mountains to steal sheep and cows from ranchos were ruthless, and there was a great deal of ill feeling between the Spanish and the *Indios* because of violent clashes. If the man was real, he was an enemy, and she and Teresita and Miguel were in danger.

There he was again! Josefina pointed and cried, "Look! A man!"

"Where?" asked Miguel, stopping short, alarmed. He turned slowly, scanning the trees. "I don't see anyone."

"Neither do I," said Teresita. She sounded very concerned as she, too, looked around them in the gathering dusk. She tightened her hold of Josefina.

"Why did you think you saw a man?" Miguel asked.

"I...I just had a feeling that we were being watched, and then, well, I saw the silhouette of a man," said Josefina uncertainly. "I guess what Santiago said frightened me."

"Perhaps the sun made the rocks cast a shadow that looked like a man," suggested Teresita, trying to calm her.

"But I also saw a bit of red," said Josefina.

"The setting sun makes the rocks glow red," said Teresita. "After all, the mountains *are* called Sangre de Cristo because they're blood-red at sunset."

"That's true," said Josefina. She tried to sound reassured. "I was dozing. Perhaps I dreamed that I saw the man. Anyway, now the shape is gone."

"Even so," said Miguel as they walked on. "I'll tell your papá that you thought you saw someone when I tell him that Santiago warned us about raiders. All of the men on the rancho will keep a vigilant eye out. We'll post lookouts on the boundaries." He sighed. "It may be that there will be trouble ahead. In any case, it's never wrong to be extra careful."

Josefina nestled back into the safety of Teresita's

arms. Teresita wrapped her soft old blanket around Josefina so that they shared its warmth. The mule, eager for its stable, walked faster, and Josefina was very glad. She, too, was eager to hurry away from the cold, darkening mountain and return to the light, warmth, and security of the hearth at home.

But somehow, no matter how quickly the mule walked, Josefina felt haunted by fear and worry; they lurked just behind her like an ominous shadow.

Because in her heart, she was quite sure she had not been dreaming. She *had* seen a man.

chapter 4

Señor Fernando

"NEIGH!" ANTONIO WHINNIED. He clucked his tongue to sound like a horse's hooves galloping on a rocky road. Then he said, "Come on, Josefina! Make your horse race mine!"

"All right!" said Josefina. "Giddyap!"

It was the next day, and Josefina, her sisters, and Antonio were in the family sala. Antonio was playing with the horse Don Javier had given him, and Josefina was keeping him company and using the horse from her toy farm while Clara and Francisca sewed. Tía Dolores and Don Javier were there, too. Tía Dolores felt a bit better today, so they'd walked up to the pasture to see Valiente, the horse that Papá was planning to sell, and now they were playing cards.

"I win," said Don Javier, fanning out his cards to show his hand.

"Oh! You've fooled me again!" said Tía Dolores. "You always *were* clever at gambling and games! You always win."

"Not always," murmured Don Javier ruefully, which made Francisca raise her eyebrows at her sisters as if to say, *He means that he lost Tía Dolores's heart to Papá!*

"How'd you manage to trick me into losing *this* time?" asked Tía Dolores.

"You were distracted by helping the girls with their mending," said Don Javier smoothly. "If you'd been paying attention, I wouldn't have won."

"I won, too!" crowed Antonio. "Or my horse did. It beat Josefina's horse in our race."

"Well done," said Don Javier.

"Now our horses must rest," said Josefina. She put her horse in the stable that was part of her toy farm. The farm was made to look like farms in the eastern

United States, far from New Mexico. It was carved
out of wood and had a tiny cow, a goat, and a funny
pink pig as well as two green trees, a white fence, and
a little white house with blue shutters.

"I'll put my horse in the house," said Antonio.
He lifted the little wooden house that was part of the
toy farm and put it over his horse. "No one will find
my horse in there."

"It will be safe," said Josefina. Miguel had spoken
to Papá, and Papá had told the servants and all the
family—except little Antonio, so as not to frighten
him—about Santiago's warning about thieves and
raiders and also about the man Josefina thought she
had seen on the mountain. Josefina thought that
right now, Miguel and Papá were probably out taking
precautions to keep *all* the creatures on the rancho as
safe as Antonio's little horse.

"Good boy," said Don Javier to Antonio. "It's
smart to hide your valuables." Josefina knew that
he was thinking about the rumors of raiders, too,

because he sounded a bit serious as he went on to say, "That little house is the perfect hiding place for keeping *anything* safe."

"And warm, too," said Antonio. "I worry that my horse must get cold. Teresita says that my horse needs a blanket like *real* horses wear when they rest. Do you think so, too, Josefina?"

"Sí," Josefina agreed. She saw Clara and Francisca exchange small, fond smiles; like Josefina, they, too, thought it was very dear that Antonio loved his toy horse so much he wanted a blanket for it!

"A blanket?" said Don Javier, shedding his brief seriousness. "Why, some horses in Mexico City wear nightgowns when they sleep. When I return there, that is, when I see all my horses again, I'll sing them to sleep with Teresita's lullaby. I love that song!" Loudly, with such great gusto that he'd *wake* horses instead of lulling them to sleep, he began to whistle the lilting tune. Tía Dolores, matching his merry mood, played it on the piano in happy harmony.

They stopped short in the middle of their music when they realized that Papá and a very handsome, well-dressed gentleman Josefina had never seen before had come into the room. Everyone stood to greet Papá and the man.

"I'm sorry to interrupt the music," said Papá. Then he turned to the man, saying, "*Por favor*, Señor Fernando, permit me to introduce my wife, Dolores; our friend, Don Javier; my daughters; and my grandson."

Tía Dolores said, "Welcome, Señor Fernando." Don Javier and Antonio bowed, and the girls clasped their hands and lowered their heads.

"Señor Fernando is from Los Cerrillos. He is an acquaintance of a businessman I met in Santa Fe," Papá explained as Señor Fernando removed his sarape and hat. "He has come because he might buy my horse Valiente, and his saddle." As was correct, Papá was getting to know Señor Fernando before they went to look at the horse and saddle. Manners came before business, always.

"Buenos días, señor y señora," said Señor Fernando in a deep and solemn voice. He nodded to Josefina, her sisters, and Antonio, saying, "Dear children." Then Señor Fernando took Tía Dolores's hand, bowed low over it, and then bowed to Don Javier. "It is a great pleasure to meet you." He put his hand over his heart as if he were overcome with emotion. "It is an honor I feel deeply, I assure you."

"Gracias, señor," said Tía Dolores. Josefina could tell that she, too, was impressed by how extremely polite Señor Fernando was. In fact, it seemed to Josefina that everything about Señor Fernando was extreme. The buttons on his short waistcoat were the brightest brass, his pants were a brilliant blue, and his eyes were as sharp as his clothes. He was compact and wiry, and he seemed to fill the room with his intensity. He looked as if he'd burst from too much pent-up energy if the blindingly red sash that circled his slender middle, just below his waistcoat, were not so tightly bound around him.

Shaking his head in sober wonder, Señor Fernando surveyed the sala. Josefina could see that he was taking in every detail of the room with admiring eyes. He flung his arms wide. "Beautiful," he pronounced in his velvety voice. He bowed low over Tía Dolores's hand again and then, nodding at her ring, he said, "A fine jewel! It is fit to grace your fine hand."

Before Señor Fernando could continue to lavish praise on everything in the sala, Papá said, "Please be seated, señor."

"Ah, yes," said Señor Fernando. "We must begin. Pleasure must give way to business." He turned to Tía Dolores. "Of course, señora, you and the children won't want to stay and be bored listening to us. Business is serious. It is of no interest to pretty señoras, *señoritas,* and babies, eh?"

Quickly, Papá said, "I beg your pardon, Señor

Fernando, my wife and my friend, Don Javier, will stay."

Señor Fernando immediately reversed his opinion and nodded slowly as if Papá had said something very, very wise. "Excelente," he said with grave approval.

"I hope you'll take some refreshment, Señor Fernando," said Tía Dolores graciously. She rose and walked over to a large wooden cupboard. She opened the cupboard door and then, using a little key she kept on a ring of keys, she unlocked a small compartment inside the cupboard and took out a silver tray. Gallantly, Señor Fernando jumped up to help her, holding the tray while she put some silver spoons, small silver cups and plates, and a silver sugar bowl and creamer on it. The silver was brightly polished, even though it was used only on special occasions when the family had honored guests.

"Gracias, Señor Fernando," said Tía Dolores. She took the tray from him and handed it to Francisca,

saying, "Girls, please take Antonio to the kitchen.
While you are there, please ask Carmen to prepare
some refreshments for Señor Fernando and bring
them to us on this tray."

"Sí, Tía Dolores," said Francisca, Clara, and
Josefina.

Francisca left with the tray. Josefina and Clara
helped Antonio gather up the pieces of the toy farm.
As they carried them to the kitchen, Antonio asked,
"Is that man one of the three kings?"

"Why, no," said Josefina. She was too kind to
laugh at Antonio's question.

"Why do you think he might be?" asked Clara.

"He seems like such an *important* person," said
Antonio, his eyes wide with awe. "And his buttons
are as shiny as gold."

"He *does* act as grand as royalty," said Josefina.
"But I think he's just a very dignified man."

"Sí," agreed Clara. "He has the fine manners of
a king."

"Well, I think he *is* one of the three kings," said Antonio stubbornly, "so I'm going to leave my shoes out during my nap today, and put hay in them, just like Juan and I did before Three Kings' Day. Then that king can leave me a gift again."

"You may if you wish," said Josefina. Antonio was bound to be disappointed, but she could see that there was no point in arguing with him!

When they got to the kitchen, Carmen was already preparing the silver tray with tea, milk, sugar, and bizcochitos. "May I serve the refreshments?" Josefina asked as she and Clara helped Antonio set up the toy farm in a corner of the kitchen. Josefina was curious, and wanted to observe what was going on in the family sala.

"Oh, yes, certainly," said Carmen. She nodded toward Antonio, who had already begun trotting his little horse around the toy farm. "Your sisters and I will keep an eye on Antonio until Teresita comes." She handed the loaded tray to Josefina.

"You be careful, and don't spill."

Slowly, Josefina carried the silver tray into the family sala and carefully placed it in front of Tía Dolores. Then she took a seat on the banco, near Tía Dolores and Don Javier. They were not part of the business discussion, but they sat quietly and listened.

Señor Fernando was just as serious and thorough with his questions as he had been with his compliments. When it came to business, Señor Fernando was obviously focused and no-nonsense. *Clara would approve*, thought Josefina as Señor Fernando asked question after question: How old was the horse Valiente? What was its pedigree? How many hands tall was it? Who trained it? Was it a balker or did it take jumps? What was its nature? It wasn't vicious, was it? Was it comfortable with mules, so that it would get along with his mule, Lucita? What was the state of its health? How much did it eat? Where was it usually kept? Did it graze freely, or was it fed in the stable yard?

Papá honestly and conscientiously answered all the questions, and then said to Señor Fernando, "*Con permiso*, shall we go to the pasture to look at Valiente now? On our way back, we can stop by the stable so that you may see his saddle in case you wish to buy that, too."

"Yes, please," said Señor Fernando. With his usual air of admiration, he said, "In fact, kind sir, if it would not be too much of an imposition, I would like to see *all* of the buildings on your rancho, not just the stable. I have recently purchased a rancho myself. This is such a splendid place: I know I would learn a great deal by observing how you have organized things here."

Papá smiled at Señor Fernando's earnest interest. "I'd be honored to give you a tour," he said.

"After your tour, we hope you will join us for our midday meal," Tía Dolores added.

"Sí, sí, sí, gracias! You are kindness itself," pronounced Señor Fernando with a sweeping bow.

"I know that I will be impressed at how well you manage such a fine property." He lowered his voice and said to Papá, "I am sure that you have heard, as I have, the rumor that there are thieves about. Are you taking extra measures to protect your house and your family?"

"Sí," said Papá. "I've posted a night guard who will circle the outside of the house once an hour, and all of our doors and windows will be securely locked."

"Very wise," said Señor Fernando.

The instant Papá, Don Javier, and Señor Fernando left to go look at Valiente, Tía Dolores and Josefina headed rather hurriedly to the kitchen. There was a great deal to do! Francisca and Clara were already helping Carmen make tortillas. "We must prepare an especially fine midday meal," said Tía Dolores, "because today we have an extra guest." She kept a close eye on Josefina as she prepared dried apples for the apple tart. Tía Dolores herself plunged her hands deep into the dough for the crust to blend the ingredients.

Josefina was proud to be of help making the tart and proud to be part of the bustle of preparation in the kitchen. She could tell that Antonio was proud, too, as he brought in an armload of sticks for the kitchen fire. Josefina smiled as she watched Antonio put a few tiny wisps of dried-up grass by the toy farm, pretending the grass was hay for his horse. Only after his toy horse had been fed did Antonio sit on a stool and eat his own meal, which Carmen had prepared for him. Antonio was too little to eat with the others in the family sala; their midday meal would be later and more formal than usual today because of Papá's guest, Señor Fernando.

Suddenly, "Oh!" said Tía Dolores with impatience. "This ring is in my way." Josefina saw Clara nudge Francisca and give her a look that said, *Didn't I tell you that ring is impractical?* Tía Dolores took off her gold-and-ruby ring, wiped it clean on a cloth, and handed it to Josefina. "Please, put this ring somewhere safe."

Francisca plucked the ring out of Josefina's hand and slid it onto her own finger. "I'll wear it!" she volunteered nobly, waving her bejeweled hand aloft, which made everyone laugh.

"She loves that ring more than Tía Dolores does," Clara muttered under her breath to Josefina. "She wishes it were hers."

"Thank you, dear Francisca," said Tía Dolores. "The ring does indeed look lovely on your beautiful hand. But I think Josefina can find a better place to store it."

Francisca plopped the ring in Josefina's hand and Josefina closed her fist around it. She searched the kitchen for a secure spot for it. Finally, her eyes lit upon the small statue, called a *bulto,* of San Pascual that sat on a shelf in a niche carved into the kitchen wall. San Pascual was the household saint who looked after cooks and kitchens. "I'll put your ring here, Tía Dolores," Josefina said, "next to the statue of

San Pascual. It will be safe. San Pascual will keep an eye on it for you." Josefina stood on her tiptoes and carefully put the ring at the feet of the bulto of San Pascual in his niche.

"Let me see!" cried Antonio. He was so enchanted that he dragged his stool over and stood on it so that his nose was practically touching the ring at the feet of the little statue.

"If you've finished eating, it is time for your nap, Antonio," said Carmen, tripping over his stool, which was very much in the way in the crowded kitchen.

"Josefina," said Tía Dolores. "Carmen has to help us bring all this food into the family sala. Will you go to the weaving room and ask Teresita to come and get Antonio for his nap?"

"Sí," said Josefina. She took some pieces of dried apple to munch on as she skipped across the court-yard to the weaving room. She poked her head in the door. *"Perdón!* Teresita?" she said. But there was no answer. Teresita wasn't there. In fact, it looked as though she had not been in the weaving room at all that day. The hanging loom was still dismantled and empty, exactly as Josefina and Teresita had left it when they'd finished the blanket for Santiago, and the bundle of carded wool that Santiago had given them was untouched.

As Josefina went back across the courtyard, she looked outside the big gate. She didn't see Teresita, but she did see Papá, Don Javier, and Señor Fernando. She could hear Señor Fernando admiring the stoutness of the outer walls and asking with awe how high they were. Josefina also saw Señor Fernando's mule, Lucita, tethered to a tree and looking lonely and forlorn. So she stepped outside the gate, and fed Lucita a bit of the dried apple she'd brought. That perked Lucita up tremendously, so Josefina fed her all the rest of the apple, singing a song and giving the mule's nose a friendly rub as she did so. Lucita sighed, as if to say, *Josefina, you are the only one who appreciates me. I work so hard. Look at the burdens I carry, and for no thanks!* Josefina grinned. In fact, Lucita's burdens did not look too awful: Though the coiled rope tied to her saddle looked heavy, her saddlebags were empty and flat. Josefina gave Lucita's ears a scratch, and then left.

When Josefina entered the kitchen, Antonio was there rearranging the animals around the toy farm. Teresita came in, right behind Josefina, seemingly blown in on the wind.

"Teresita," said Josefina, "I was just looking for you in the weaving room. Where were you?"

"Oh, I was on my way here from outside," said Teresita breezily. She brushed past Josefina, scooped Antonio up into her arms, kissed him on his chubby cheek, and smilingly carried him off to take his nap. *Antonio reminds Teresita of her brother, Níyol,* thought Josefina. *How nice that must be for Teresita.*

Josefina lingered in the kitchen to wash her hands and tidy herself up a bit before she went to the family sala. She thought that because of that delay, she'd be the last one to come to the meal, but in fact, Don Javier arrived at the same time she did, slipping quietly into the room with her. He had a sly expression, as if he had been up to trickery, as he sat down on the banco.

When Tía Dolores passed him a plate, Don Javier remarked, "Why, Dolores, you aren't wearing your ring." Josefina couldn't tell if he was *pretending* to have hurt feelings, or if he really *was* hurt when he went on to say with a very long face, "Do you mean that after all the trouble I went to in order to bring the ring to you, you are tired of it already?"

"No, no, no," said Tía Dolores. "I took it off because I was getting dough all over it. But don't worry. Josefina placed it safely at the feet of the bulto of San Pascual in the kitchen."

"A good place," said Señor Fernando judiciously. "Such a valuable ring must be kept safe. I saw on my tour how conscientious you are about security here. Exemplary!"

When Señor Fernando finished his meal, he touched his lips with the edge of his linen napkin, and then said with a heavy sigh, "It grieves me, but I must climb on my mule Lucita and go now."

"Oh, won't you stay this afternoon and tonight?" said Papá. "We'd be pleased."

"I, too, would be pleased beyond words," said Señor Fernando. "And so would Lucita. But alas, it is not for us to do as we please in this world, is it? I must go to Los Cerrillos to collect the money I will need to buy your fine horse, Señor Montoya. Indeed, indeed, Valiente is the finest horse in New Mexico, I believe. So, though I am sad to go, my consolation is that I will return soon to buy Valiente, and of course, that means I will have the honor and pleasure of seeing you and your lovely wife and Don Javier again. Oh," he added swiftly, "and your enchanting children, of course."

He smiled widely at the sisters. Clara blushed, looking pleased, but Francisca seemed less impressed.

She was complimented on her beauty so frequently that she took compliments rather for granted!

Bowing, smiling sadly, and still talking in a mournful way about how sorry he was to leave, Señor Fernando left the family sala, moving with a smooth and agile grace. After a short stop in the kitchen to thank Carmen for the delicious meal, he mounted Lucita. He had to prod Lucita to move with much loud encouragement. The mule seemed reluctant to budge and even more melancholy about leaving the rancho than Señor Fernando claimed to be.

As Josefina and her sisters were stacking the plates to bring them from the family sala to the kitchen, Francisca took a napkin and imitated Señor Fernando dabbing at his lips. "Indeed, indeed," she said in Señor Fernando's very ponderous manner, "all through dinner I was so sorry that I had to leave that I was only able to eat four tortillas and two pieces of apple tart. Alas, alas."

"Francisca!" scolded Clara. "You mustn't make fun of Señor Fernando. It's disrespectful. He has beautiful manners."

"He reminds me of a rooster," said Francisca. "And if he's such a fancy horse trader, why does he ride that fat old mule?"

"I like Lucita!" Josefina asserted. "We're friends."

"Mule or no mule, no matter what he rides, Señor Fernando is a *gentleman*," said Clara. "He is thoroughly proper and polite. You see that, don't you, Josefina?"

"Yes," said Josefina. It seemed to her that everything Señor Fernando had said and done had been perfect. He was overflowing with praise and appreciation, saying how much he wished he could stay. She asked, "I wonder why he had to go back to Los Cerrillos? Surely he could have brought the money with him to buy Papá's horse."

"I'm sure that he has heard the rumor that thieves may be about," said Francisca. "He probably wanted to see Valiente first, to be sure he wanted to buy him. No one wants to carry money on the road until he *has* to."

"In any case, it would have been rude to talk to Papá about money today," said Clara. "It's good manners to get to know someone before doing business with him, and Señor Fernando's manners are impeccable."

"Exemplary!" Francisca said in her Señor Fernando voice.

"Very," said Josefina.

"Well, *I* am glad Señor Fernando's gone!" said Francisca in her own voice, heaving an exaggerated sigh. "Extra guests are extra work."

"Then you'll be glad that Don Javier is leaving, too," said Clara. "I heard him tell Papá that he has an important errand to do. He's going to Cordero for a few days, to see an acquaintance who lives there. He'll come back here before he returns to Mexico City."

"When is he leaving?" asked Francisca.

"Today," said Clara.

"*Today?*" repeated Francisca. "How soon?"

"He and Tía Dolores were in the kitchen a minute ago. She was packing saddlebags of food for him to take with him," said Clara. "I imagine that as soon as the saddlebags are ready, Don Javier will go."

"Quick!" said Francisca, rushing to the window. "He may already be leaving."

The three girls squeezed together to look out the window. Sure enough, Don Javier was mounting his horse. As they watched, Papá and Don Javier shook hands. Then Don Javier leaned down, took the saddlebags from Tía Dolores, and settled them onto his horse. He said thank you and good-bye to Tía Dolores, looking uncharacteristically serious. Then he straightened, his shoulders stiff. Josefina thought that he didn't seem at all like his usual high-spirited, playful self as he rode away, accompanied by his manservant and one of the rancho servants for safety. *Perhaps Don Javier is worried he will encounter raiders on his journey,* Josefina thought, *or perhaps he's nervous about the errand he is going to do.* She watched as he grew smaller and smaller in the distance, noticing that the edges of his red scarf fluttered like tiny tattered flags behind his back.

chapter 5

The Ring Is Gone

JOSEFINA AND HER sisters gathered in the family sala to tidy it after the midday meal. Tía Dolores had given Clara the little key to the locked compartment in the cupboard, and Francisca was helping Clara put the silver away. Josefina was sweeping crumbs from the floor. It was quiet now that all their guests were gone. Peaceful afternoon sunshine slanted through the slats of the windows, and the hearth fire's warmth was gentle. *I am sure that this quietness is what Tía Dolores needs to restore her energy*, thought Josefina. *Having all the guests has exhausted her.*

She looked up with a smile as Tía Dolores hurried into the sala. But her smile quickly disappeared when she saw Tía Dolores's worried face.

"My ring," said Tía Dolores, her voice unusually tense and tight. "Have any of you seen my ring?"

The sisters looked up. No one answered.

Tía Dolores spoke deliberately, going back over the facts as she explained. "I realized that I didn't put my ring back on after the midday meal," she said. "So just now, I went to the kitchen to get it. I looked for the ring in the niche by San Pascual, but it wasn't there. Neither Carmen nor Miguel has it. Do any of you?"

"No," said the sisters all together.

"Josefina," said Francisca, "Tía Dolores gave it to you to put aside safely. You were the last one who had it."

"Sí," said Josefina, "but I haven't seen it since I put it by San Pascual, in his niche."

"That's where I last saw it, too," said Tía Dolores, agitated, "but I looked and looked just now and my ring is *not* there. The Glowing Heart ring is *gone*."

"I'm sure your ring has just been mislaid,"

Josefina said. "Let's all go to the kitchen and look for it."

Hurriedly, Clara locked the door to the small compartment inside the cupboard and gave the little key back to Tía Dolores. Then they all rushed to the kitchen.

A hundred times—a *thousand* times—Josefina searched San Pascual's niche. She lifted the little statue and felt all around the niche with her hand. She knelt and searched the floor below the niche, sticking her hands in every tiny crack. Clara sifted the ashes on the hearth, in case the ring had somehow fallen into the fire. Francisca dusted every shelf and looked into every jar and pot. Carmen swept every inch of the floor, but other than the usual dust, all she swept away was the grass Antonio had scattered at the toy farm, which was in a corner of the kitchen. Tía Dolores looked under the table, under the stools, under the blanket that was spread on the banco, and under the sticks stacked next to the fire.

No one could find the ring.

Tía Dolores's shoulders sagged. With all her heart, Josefina wanted to help. Where else could the ring be? Josefina thought hard. At last she said, "Oh! I have an idea! Tía Dolores, maybe the ring fell off the shelf and rolled into the crack where the wall meets the floor behind the tall green chest."

"Maybe," Tía Dolores said with a shrug. "We might as well look."

The sisters exchanged glances. Never before had they heard Tía Dolores sound so tired and so without hope. They'd just started to push against the heavy chest, trying to shove it a few inches out from the wall, when Papá appeared. "Dolores!" he exclaimed with concern. Swiftly, he rushed to her. "What are you doing?"

"We're searching for my ring," said Tía Dolores. "It isn't in its niche." Tía Dolores's face was pale. "I've lost my Glowing Heart ring."

"I'm sorry," said Papá. Gently, he pulled her

away from the chest. "Of course you must look for it. But you must let me move anything as heavy as this tall green chest for you. Promise me that you will."

"*Yo te prometo*," said Tía Dolores. "I promise."

Papá pushed the chest forward, away from the wall. With more determination than hope, Josefina and her sisters got on their hands and knees, looking closely at every inch of the exposed floor. Josefina ran her fingers along the crack where the wall met the floor. She found nothing.

Josefina sat back on her folded legs. She shook her head. "I'm sorry," she said.

Papá pushed the tall green chest back, and Tía Dolores sighed. Papá put his arm around her shoulders. "Come now, my love," he said to Tía Dolores. "You're tired. You'll feel better if you lie down and rest for a while before dinner." He smiled. "I need a rest, too. Señor Fernando exhausted me. He was curious about *everything*. He asked, How many servants are there? When do they get up in the morning? Where is our family altar?" Papá shook his head. "I've never had such an interested and attentive guest before, or one with more questions."

"Or compliments," added Tía Dolores.

"He was indeed lavish with his praise," said Papá. He urged Tía Dolores forward, saying, "The girls will help you search for your ring again tomorrow, when the kitchen is full of sunlight. Won't you, my daughters?"

"Sí, Papá," said all the sisters.

"Bless you, children," said Papá. "I'm sure the ring will be found."

Papá's strong voice was calm and reassuring. But as he and Tía Dolores left the kitchen, Josefina said a silent prayer to San Antonio, the patron saint of lost objects. As hard as she could, she prayed, "Help us, San Antonio. Help us find the Glowing Heart ring for Tía Dolores."

Francisca's voice cut into her silent prayer. "Well!" said Francisca.

"Well, what?" asked Clara, rubbing the dust off her hands with a cloth.

"*Well*," said Francisca, who always was eager to stir up romantic fires. "Papá is pampering Tía Dolores because he can see that she isn't happy. She misses Don Javier already."

Clara sniffed dismissively. "No, she's unhappy about losing her ring. I don't blame her. Where *is* that ring? We've turned the kitchen upside down looking for it!" Clara turned to Josefina. "You've looked especially hard, Josefina. Aren't you beginning to suspect that the ring has been stolen?"

"Stolen?" repeated Josefina, horrified. "Oh, no! It's only *lost*. We just haven't found it yet."

"You want to think so because you never like to think that anyone is bad," said Clara, not unkindly, "and if the ring is stolen, it means that someone is a thief."

"No one we know would do such a thing," said
Josefina, hoping with all her heart that what she said
was true.

"Stop being such a silly old sourpuss, Clara,"
said Francisca. "Next thing you'll say is that *I* stole
Tía Dolores's ring because I like it so much."

"You did try it on," said Clara, "and you were
more enraptured with it than Tía Dolores was."

Francisca fluttered her graceful fingers. "If I had
stolen the Glowing Heart ring, I'd be wearing it,"
she said. "After all, it looked exquisite on my hand.
And have you ever known me to be shy about show-
ing off?"

"Never!" said Josefina and Clara together.

Josefina looked out the window. Dusk began
to darken the sky, and suspicions began to darken
Josefina's mind. Slowly, reluctantly, without facing
her sisters, she asked, "If the ring *was* stolen, who
could the thief be?"

"Don Javier was in the kitchen when Tía Dolores

was preparing the food for him to take on his journey," said Clara. "Maybe when she wasn't looking, Don Javier took the ring to teach Tía Dolores a lesson. He acted hurt when he saw that she was not wearing it. Maybe he plans to deceive her. He'll keep the ring for a while to show her how bad she'd feel if the ring were gone, and then he'll give it back."

"Or maybe he took it to show her how bad it feels to lose something you love, the way *he* lost *her*," suggested Francisca. "He wants her heart to be broken, as his is."

"Either way, it is a deception," said Clara crisply. "And it is a sin and a shame for Don Javier to tease poor Tía Dolores like that, and to upset her. I *told* you he's not to be trusted."

"Well, but Señor Fernando was in the kitchen, too," said Francisca, "when he said thank you to Carmen."

"Which was polite and proper for him to do," interrupted Clara.

"Maybe when Carmen wasn't looking, Señor Fernando took the ring," said Francisca.

Josefina said, "I *did* think that his story about having to go to Los Cerrillos was a bit peculiar, no matter what you say, Clara, about how it would not have been proper manners to complete his business with Papá on the first day they met."

"Maybe Señor Fernando left so immediately because he stole the ring," said Francisca. "Though he'd hardly make a quick getaway on that disagreeable mule, Lucita!"

"Poor Lucita," murmured Josefina with sympathy.

"Señor Fernando is far too superior to steal!" exclaimed Clara, outraged. "Didn't Papá say he'd never had such an attentive guest before? And didn't you see how Señor Fernando helped Tía Dolores and held the heavy silver tray for her, like a gentleman? Why, he's so dignified that Antonio thinks that he's one of the three kings!"

"Well, if it isn't Don Javier, and it isn't Señor Fernando, then who is the thief?" said Francisca.

"Maybe," said Josefina, "the rumor Santiago heard was true and there *are* thieves and raiders around. I'm pretty sure that I did see a man on the mountain. What if he is a raider who planned to sneak down to the rancho to steal livestock? Do you think there's any way he could have sneaked into the kitchen and stolen Tía Dolores's ring?"

"No!" said Clara. "He'd have been seen by a guard."

"Unless he's invisible, like a ghost," said Francisca.

Josefina shuddered. Francisca came up behind her and put her hands on her shoulders. "What's the matter, little sister?" she asked. "Has all this talk about guards and ghosts and thieves upset you?"

"Sí," admitted Josefina.

"*Lo siento*," said Clara. "I'm sorry." She sighed. Sounding gentler and sweeter than usual, she said,

"We're all on edge because of the threat of raiders. And I think we're all unhappy, too, because Tía Dolores is unhappy."

"Heartbroken," Francisca corrected her, "not just unhappy."

Josefina listened to her sisters. She didn't know which one of them was right, or even if *either* of them was right. But she was sure that whatever Papá did must be right. So she resolved to do as he was doing: help Tía Dolores. She might not be able to figure out what had happened to Tía Dolores's ring, or to find the thief—assuming there was one. But it cheered her to think that she *could* make life on the rancho as easy and pleasant for Tía Dolores as possible.

Josefina put her plan into action the very next morning. Even though she loved cooking with Tía Dolores, Josefina wanted to ease her workload, so when Tía Dolores invited her to make pumpkin *empanadas,* Josefina said, "Oh, gracias, but Carmen and I can make the empanadas. You needn't trouble yourself."

"But," Tía Dolores began. She stopped and just nodded. "Very well," she said. "As you wish. I'll go help Clara and Francisca dust the sleeping salas."

Josefina felt regretful, because Tía Dolores sounded more sorry than relieved. And oh, dear! All too soon, Josefina was sorry, too.

Cooking *without* Tía Dolores wasn't as much fun as cooking with her, and cooking with Antonio underfoot—since Carmen was too busy cooking with Josefina to distract him—wasn't fun at all. Josefina hoped he'd be quiet and out of the way when he was playing with his toy horse and the toy farm. The toy farm had taken up permanent residence in a corner of the kitchen ever since she and Clara had helped Antonio put it there yesterday before the midday meal. Antonio kept begging Josefina to join him and play with it. After the twentieth time, Josefina asked

him, exasperated, "Aren't you supposed to be helping Teresita sweep the weaving room this morning?"

"She isn't there," said Antonio. "Look, Josefina!
See my horse's red blanket. Isn't it fine?"

"Mm-hmm," murmured Josefina. She was filling
the empanadas, which was tricky because if she used
too much mashed pumpkin, the empanada burst.
Too little, and it was flat as a squashed bug.

"Look!" Antonio demanded.

So Josefina glanced up. She was surprised to
see that Antonio's toy horse did indeed have a red
blanket—a scrap of red woven cloth—tied around
it. "My! What a handsome blanket," said Josefina.
"Where did you get it? Did Teresita give it to you?"

"No," said Antonio reverently. "The king did."

"The king?" asked Josefina.

"Sí!" said Antonio. "Yesterday, I put my shoes
out during my nap, and the king left this gift for me.
He's the king who rides his mule Lucita instead of
a camel."

"The king who—? Oh, you mean Señor Fernando," said Josefina. She didn't want to crush Antonio's sweet imagination, but it seemed extremely unlikely to her that somber, serious Señor Fernando had gone to the trouble of leaving a surprise present for Antonio. Francisca, Clara, Tía Dolores, and Don Javier had all been in the family sala when Antonio told them that Teresita had said that his horse needed a blanket. Surely, the scrap of red cloth was secretly from one of them. Or was it from Teresita? Josefina would ask her first.

"Carmen," Josefina asked, "do you know where Teresita is? Antonio says she isn't in the weaving room."

Carmen looked fretful. "You know Teresita," she said. "I *reminded* her that Miguel warned us about thieves and raiders. I *told* her to stay close to the rancho. But she wouldn't listen to me. She's so excited about that bundle of carded wool that Santiago gave you that she insisted on going out to gather bark and roots to make dyes. She says no one's better at finding plants to make the dyes than she is, even in the winter." She shivered. "I prefer to stay safe and warm by the kitchen fire."

Even though Josefina understood that Teresita hadn't invited her to go on the root-and-bark-gathering expedition because of the danger of raiders nearby, she was a little hurt. "Teresita knows that I love those expeditions," Josefina said to Carmen. "She said that I was her best helper at spotting plants to make dyes, and that I could go with her next time."

"Dear child," said Carmen, "thank goodness you didn't! Then I'd have been worried sick about both of you! Besides, you can't be in two places at once. Teresita knows you're busy helping me with the baking. And right now, you had better grab those empanadas. All this chatter has distracted you and now they're burning!"

"Oh, no!" wailed Josefina. Quickly, she pulled the

empanadas out of the small oven next to the hearth. Sure enough, Carmen was right: The empanadas were burned on the bottom. Josefina *had* been distracted, and not just by the chatter, but also by a nagging worry about Teresita. Was she in danger right now? Why hadn't she even *told* Josefina that she was going to look for roots and bark? Where had she been yesterday when Josefina had looked for her in the weaving room? Teresita had always been so steady and reliable, and now, suddenly, yesterday and today, she was elusive. Her odd behavior couldn't possibly have anything to do with the lost ring, could it? No! Teresita would never take anything that did not belong to her. Josefina put any such suspicion out of her head.

Instead, she looked at the burned empanadas and sighed, saying, "Tía Dolores always says, 'The saints cry over lost time.' I'm sure that they cry over wasted food, too. I'll wait for these ruined empanadas to cool, and then I'll feed them to Sombrita and the other goats." Josefina's pet goat, Sombrita, and the other goats had already enjoyed eating the worst of her too-thick tortillas and too-thin bizcochitos. "I'm sorry, Carmen."

"Never mind," said Carmen kindly. "I've been cooking since long before you were born and I still make mistakes. You'll do better next time."

"I hope so!" said Josefina. Some of the empanadas weren't too bad, but others were so burned that they were stuck to the pan. Josefina tried to scrape the pan clean, but the burned bits were stubborn.

"You'd better take that pan to the stream right away," said Carmen. "There are workers in the field nearby, so you'll be safe. Soak that pan and scrub it clean."

"May I come, too?" asked Antonio immediately.

"Sí," said Josefina. "Come along." She picked up the pan in one hand, and held the other hand out to Antonio. "Hold my hand on the way, and stay close when we're at the stream."

Antonio pulled Josefina's hand to make her walk faster out the door and down the path, saying, "Giddyap!" as he galloped his toy horse through the air so that its red blanket fluttered.

chapter 6

Who Was at the Stream?

THOUGH THE SUN shone strong in a daz-
zlingly blue sky, it was a bone-chilling winter day.
The water in the stream, cold as liquid snow, soon
numbed Josefina's hands as she scrubbed the burned
pan. Usually Josefina lingered at the stream, but
today Santiago's warning made her feel jumpy. Even
though she was determined not to give in to her fear,
and even though she knew that workers were within
shouting distance, she hurried.

Swoosh, swoosh. Josefina dunked the pan in the
water that rushed over the shiny pebbles. The stream
cheered her with its rushing song as it slipped along,
over and around shiny rocks, sparkling in the sunshine. Antonio was happily occupied. He pretended
that his toy horse was drinking from the stream and

splashing in it, which meant that Antonio was getting rather wet, but Josefina thought it would do him no harm. Above, a merry-sounding bird softly whistled a sweet trill. Josefina whistled back, echoing the trill. Then it seemed as if the bird's whistle turned into a tune. Josefina cocked her head. Strangely, she seemed to recognize the tune. As the soft whistling continued, Josefina held still and held her breath so that she could hear it clearly. How odd! The whistler wasn't a bird at all. It was a person. Someone was whistling Teresita's lullaby, the tune behind the words:

> *Softly may you sleep now,*
> *Softly may you sleep.*

Who could it be? Then Josefina smiled. Of course! The whistler must be Don Javier! Didn't he say he loved the tune? Josefina remembered how he had whistled it so loudly yesterday. Don Javier had said he'd be in Cordero for three days, but how nice that he was back already.

"Don Javier!" Josefina called out. "Hello?"

The whistling stopped immediately. Not a twig moved, but Josefina saw a wisp—just the quickest, merest flicker of red—whisk by between the tree trunks and then fly off in the direction of Arroyo Blanco.

Josefina laughed and called out, "It's no use running off. I saw your red scarf, Don Javier." It was just like that trickster Don Javier to try to fool her. As Clara said, he loved to be sneaky.

But Don Javier didn't respond. The only sound was a whisper of wind, blowing across the stream toward Arroyo Blanco. Josefina shivered. Suddenly, she was shaken by the same spooky feeling she'd had on the mountain. She felt as if someone had been watching her. It was someone who had moved as swiftly as a bird, someone who had not wanted her to see him, someone who had disappeared into invisibility, just as the man on the mountain had. And it was someone who knew Teresita's lullaby.

But who could it be, if it was not Don Javier?

"Why're you calling Don Javier?" Antonio asked, jolting Josefina back into the moment.

"I thought I heard him whistling," said Josefina. "I bet he's playing one of his jokes on us." Josefina stood. As she dried the scrubbed pan with a cloth, she winked at Antonio and called out, "All right, Don Javier. Antonio and I won't tell anyone that I heard you whistling here at the stream, or that you're back from Cordero. You can appear as if by magic and surprise everyone, as you love to do!"

"But you won't surprise *us*!" crowed Antonio to the invisible Don Javier.

"That's right," said Josefina. "Come, Antonio. I'll race you back to the house."

Josefina ran a little bit ahead of Antonio, keeping a sharp pace up the hill from the stream. It felt wonderful to run. The cold wind pushed against her back, propelling her up the hill. When she reached the crest, breathless and chilled, she stopped, turned, and looked back toward Antonio. As she turned, she saw a figure in the distance. It was Teresita, wearing her old blanket with the red fringe, walking toward the house along the path that led directly to and from Arroyo Blanco. It occurred to Josefina that the whistler at the stream had run off in the direction of Arroyo Blanco. Teresita must have passed him, so she would know for sure whether the whistler was Don Javier. Josefina decided to wait for Teresita to ask her.

As she waited, Josefina began to think. It struck her as odd that Teresita had chosen Arroyo Blanco for her gathering expedition. Teresita herself had told Josefina that the arroyo was called "blanco" because it was so dry that it was blanched white, so it was not at all a good place to go to look for roots and herbs to make dyes. And in fact, as Teresita came closer, Josefina saw that Teresita's hands were empty. She had no basket or sack for carrying any gathered roots or bark. So why *had* Teresita gone to Arroyo Blanco?

Josefina's breath caught in her throat as, unbidden, an ugly thought slithered into her mind: Had Teresita lied to Carmen? Had she gone to Arroyo Blanco for some secret purpose? Teresita was bent forward, scuttling along in a hurry. She looked as though she didn't want to be seen, but she didn't look afraid. Arroyo Blanco was so twisted, its sides so pocked with caves and crannies, that it would be a perfect place for a raider to hide. Wasn't Teresita nervous about going there alone at this time of heightened danger?

"I win!" shouted Antonio as he trotted past Josefina. "Why'd you stop?"

"I'm waiting for Teresita," said Josefina. "You wait, too."

"Oh, please, no," begged Antonio. He came back, took Josefina's hand, and tugged her forward. "I got all sopping wet at the stream so I'm *freezing*. Please, help me change."

Antonio did indeed look blue with cold, and his little hand felt cold as ice. "All right," said Josefina.

She allowed Antonio to pull her toward the house.
I'll ask Teresita all my questions later, she thought.
Josefina was sure that Teresita's answers would shine
a light that would end her shadowy worries.

But Josefina missed her chance to speak to
Teresita. It took a while to wrangle Antonio out of
his wet clothes, rub him dry, and help him change
into warm, dry clothes and shoes and socks. By the
time Josefina and Antonio got to the kitchen, where
everyone was starting to prepare the midday meal,
Carmen said that Teresita had been there and left
already. Josefina had to tuck her troublesome questions away for a while; she couldn't go looking for
Teresita because she had to help get the meal ready.
It would be a simpler meal than the day before: no
special apple tart, no shining, special-occasion sil-
verware, no honored guests, no formality. Without
getting in Carmen's way, Josefina looked for the

ruined empanadas to feed to Sombrita and the other goats. She looked high and low, but she couldn't find them anywhere. She asked Carmen, Tía Dolores, and her sisters, but no one said she'd thrown them away. "Antonio," Josefina asked, "did you eat those over-baked empanadas?"

"No," said Antonio. He looked up from putting his little carved toy horse in the toy stable, his face bright with hope. "Are we going to make another Kings' Cake and hide the ring in it soon?"

"No, not until next Three Kings' Day," said Josefina kindly. She remembered how difficult it was to wait for special days when you were little. She also remembered how excited Antonio had been about the hidden ring. She didn't want to make him sad by telling him that the ring had disappeared. "Do you want to help me make empanadas now?"

"Can we hide things in them?" asked Antonio. "And have a party?"

"No, I'm afraid not," Josefina said. "These are just

for our meal, which won't be a party like yesterday. But you can help me put mashed pumpkin in these empanadas, and try not to spill too much. It might be messy."

"Well, all right," said Antonio, who always loved doing anything that might be messy!

Even though Josefina worked painstakingly and this batch of empanadas turned out perfectly, she noticed that Tía Dolores just nibbled at hers. In fact, Tía Dolores ate very little of the meal at all. Indeed, there were lots of empanadas left over, because Don Javier did *not* appear.

Then who was the whistler at the stream? Josefina puzzled. Papá had just finished saying that he and Miguel had been in the pastures repairing a fence all morning, so it could not have been either of them. Tía Dolores, Clara, and Francisca had spent the morning together dusting the sleeping salas. Who else knew the tune? Señor Fernando had overheard it yesterday when Don Javier was whistling it in the family sala and Tía Dolores was playing it on the piano. But Señor Fernando was in Los Cerrillos, wasn't he? He was away, just as Don Javier was away.

Josefina toyed with her food, worrying about whether or not she should tell Papá about the whistler. But what would be the use if she did? It would only upset everyone. And how could she tell Papá about the whistler without saying that whoever he was, he knew the tune of Teresita's lullaby? That connected the whistler to Teresita, so then she'd have to tell Papá about seeing Teresita coming from Arroyo Blanco today, and her odd disappearance yesterday. Would Papá think that Teresita had been sneaking off to meet the whistler, that the whistled tune was a signal they'd agreed upon? That would mean that the whistler was someone Teresita knew but had to keep secret for some—Josefina swallowed hard—terrible reason. What could the reason be? Josefina dreaded the idea of asking Teresita that question and all her other questions, too. Her heart sank at the same time that her determination rose to clear up the puzzle of Teresita's odd behavior. Then she had an inspiration: *I'll go to Arroyo Blanco this very afternoon,* she resolved, *to see what's happening there. Maybe I can find out why Teresita went there without asking her all of my horrible, prying questions.*

As the girls cleared the table, Francisca said, "Did you notice that Tía Dolores hardly touched her meal? It's just as I told you. She misses Don Javier."

"No," said Clara. "It's as *I* told *you*. She's upset about her ring."

"We're *all* upset," said Josefina, trying to make peace.

"Yes, Josefina," said Clara. "I notice that you hardly ate anything, either. You left as much on your plate as Tía Dolores did."

Josefina had an idea. Clara had given her the excuse she needed to justify going to Arroyo Blanco. Josefina held her hands to her stomach. "My stomach is a bit upset," she said. That was true; her stomach had been tied in a knot ever since Tía Dolores's ring disappeared. It was even worse now that she was so confused by—and suspicious of—Teresita. "This afternoon, I'll go into the hills with Miguel and gather fresh sagebrush leaves to make tea. Sagebrush tea will settle Tía Dolores's digestion and mine. It will help us feel better."

"Good!" said Francisca, "then we'll *all* feel better."

Josefina stood on the top of the hill above Arroyo Blanco. Below her, the narrow, nearly flat floor of the arroyo was dry. Water had cut the deep, zigzagging gulch between the two steep sides, but no water had run through the arroyo for a long time now, not since the flood. Josefina closed her eyes and tilted her head back so that the sun shone full on her face. In spite of all her worries, as always when she stood in this high spot, Josefina felt refreshed. She opened her eyes and looked around herself, exhilarated by the endless expanse of blue sky overhead, and the gusty breeze that zipped around her and made her skirt billow out. The breeze seemed to blow the cloudy thoughts out of her head, and sun and sky filled her with hope that all would be well. She remembered the words of a psalm that her loving Mamá had taught her: *I will lift up mine eyes unto the hills, from whence cometh my help.* Josefina felt a new determination to find out what had happened; she promised herself that she wouldn't give in to hopelessness, no matter how the worry of the stolen ring, Tía Dolores's lassitude, Teresita's unusual behavior, and the threat of raiders tugged at her. She wouldn't let those worries overcome her— but she would not forget them, either.

How could she? Reminders were everywhere. For example, Miguel was close by. Josefina had never been allowed to leave the rancho by herself, but now, with the rumor that there were raiders around, Miguel was *especially* vigilant for her safety. He also was on the lookout for sheep. Sometimes sheep straggled behind the flock or wandered away and got lost on the hills or fell into an arroyo. It was important to find them and rescue them. So Miguel was on the lookout for raiders and strays, while Josefina was on the lookout for sagebrush leaves. Her godmother, Tía Magdalena, was a respected *curandera*, or healer, in the village and Josefina wanted to be one, too, when she grew up. Tía Magdalena had taught Josefina that sagebrush leaves made a bitter tea that, when sweetened with honey, was a trusted brew to soothe an upset digestion.

As she collected sagebrush leaves, Josefina thought hard. The person she had seen and heard at the stream this morning had run off in this direction. What if some unknown thief had stolen Tía Dolores's ring, and that thief was now hiding out in Arroyo Blanco, planning to come back and steal something else? Maybe Josefina had unwittingly ruined his plan when she'd heard him at the stream earlier, and now he was lurking, waiting for another chance to come down to the rancho and steal. Arroyo Blanco would be a good place for hiding.

Hiding.

Josefina did not like to think much about her other reason for coming to Arroyo Blanco: to find out what secret Teresita was hiding. It made Josefina's heart ache to even consider that Teresita had anything to do with the disappearance of Tía Dolores's ring. Why would Teresita steal the ring? She could never wear it, never flaunt it or "show it off," as Francisca had said that she would. Nor could Teresita sell the ring anywhere near the rancho, the village, or even Santa Fe, because word would be sure to get back to Papá or Abuelito if she did. *Ah,* a whisper hissed in Josefina's brain, *but what if Teresita had a helper, an accomplice, a partner in crime? What if Teresita had told him about the ring, and taught him the lullaby so that they could use it as a secret signal? What if the accomplice had come to the stream this morning to meet Teresita there so that she could give him the ring she had stolen?* That person could sell the ring for Teresita somewhere far away like Albuquerque and split the money with Teresita, and then Teresita could use the money to run away.

Josefina shaded her eyes from the sun and looked into the arroyo. Was a clue to Teresita's innocence— or guilt—hidden in the arroyo's depths, around one of its abrupt corners? Why had Josefina seen Teresita coming from here? Had Teresita mistakenly come here to Arroyo Blanco to meet someone, while he had gone to the stream to meet her? But the arroyo gave up no clues. Except for the invisible wind that whisked its way through the twists and turns, the arroyo was empty, lifeless, and colorless.

Or was it?

Something bright red caught Josefina's eye. Surely no flowers were blooming now, in the hard cold of January? But Josefina definitely saw something red, caught on a branch that stuck out from the side of the arroyo not far below her feet. She bent to look more

closely. It was a frayed twist of red wool. How did
it get there? Her curiosity piqued, Josefina squatted,
and then leaned forward to reach for the red wool.
Suddenly, the dry land crumbled under Josefina's
feet, the edge collapsed, and Josefina fell. *Down, down,
down* she slid on her back, too shocked and surprised
even to call out. Desperate to slow her descent, she
twisted so that she faced the wall of the arroyo, wildly
grabbing at tufts of grass, but they came away in her
hand. The clumps of dirt she grabbed turned to dust
so that she couldn't stop herself.

Then, with a sickening *thump*, Josefina landed
feet first on a narrow ledge sticking out from
the bank of the arroyo. For a moment—scraped,
bumped, and bruised—all she could do was fight
to catch her breath. Then, "Miguel?" she croaked.
But the wind had been knocked out of her. She
was too breathless, her throat too choked with
dust, to call out with enough strength for Miguel
to hear her.

When she had calmed herself, Josefina realized that the ledge she was standing on was part of a narrow path that stuck out from the sharply vertical bank of the arroyo. The path wound down to the bottom of the arroyo to her right and up to the top of the arroyo to her left. Inching her way along, Josefina began to walk up the path. She ran one hand along the wall of the arroyo as she made her way toward the top. On the way, she plucked the red wool from the branch and studied it. It was bright and dry; it had not been exposed to wind and sun for long.

Who'd hiked down to the bottom of the arroyo recently, and whose clothes had been caught accidentally as he—or she—had passed the branch sticking out from the side of the trail? Hadn't Josefina seen Teresita coming from Arroyo Blanco this morning, and hadn't she been wearing her blanket with the red fringe? Teresita, who was always so busy and purposeful, surely had not come to the arroyo for no reason, and yet, Arroyo Blanco was too dry a place to look for roots or herbs to make dyes. Indeed, when Josefina had seen her, Teresita had been carrying no basket or gathering sack anyway. Had she gone to Arroyo Blanco to meet a partner in crime? *No!* Josefina said to herself. *I do **not** want to suspect Teresita! Couldn't someone else have snagged his clothes?* Josefina saw that the red wool could be from Don Javier's scarf; it had looked tattered and torn when she saw it last. Or it could be from Señor Fernando's sash. It was red, too, wasn't it? And hadn't Josefina seen a flash of red when she'd spotted, ever so fleetingly, the wraithlike man on the mountain on the way home from Santiago's hut?

Josefina's hand was scratched and trembling as she carefully tucked the twist of wool inside her sash. But a little thing like a tumble that had injured her hand wasn't going to stop her from finding the answers to all her questions. She climbed to the top of the arroyo, dusted off her clothes, rubbed the smudges off her elbows and knees, and went to find

Miguel so that they could go home. Señor Fernando
and Don Javier were gone or hiding, so she could
not ask them about the red wool, and the man on the
mountain had disappeared into thin air. But, unpleas-
ant as it might be to question someone she loved
and admired so much, she was determined to speak
to Teresita, to find out the truth about her guilt or
innocence.

Josefina found Teresita and Antonio in the
weaving room. As always, the serenity of the room
calmed her. Even Antonio was quiet as he played
with a ball of wool. Teresita, kneeling in front of the
hanging loom, turned to Josefina and smiled, her
face wreathed in wrinkles of good humor. Josefina
smiled back with fondness for Teresita; how good it
was going to feel to speak openly to Teresita and free
her mind of its questions! The weaving room was
the perfect place to do so. It was here, in this very

room, that Teresita had lovingly and patiently taught Josefina to weave, a skill that had brought Josefina pleasure—and pride, too, because it enabled her to help her family. And it was in this room that Teresita had comforted Josefina by reminding her that though they had both lost their beloved mamás at a young age, they would never forget them but would always carry them in their hearts.

Josefina knelt next to Teresita. She held out her hand, palm up, with the piece of red wool on it. "Look, Teresita," she said. "I found this caught on a branch along a trail that led to the bottom of Arroyo Blanco."

Teresita looked at the wool and then lifted her dark eyes to meet Josefina's. She said nothing.

Josefina didn't want to be rude but, driven to unravel all the mysteries that were troubling the rancho, she had to go on. With a voice full of respect and affection for Teresita, she said, "I wonder if this red wool came off the fringe of your favorite blanket?

I ask because I saw you coming from Arroyo Blanco this morning. I was on my way back from the stream, where I'd gone to scrub a pan because I burned a batch of empanadas on it. I was surprised to see you; we're all supposed to stay close to home because of the threat of raiders. It was brave of you to be out alone. Please, will you tell me why you went to Arroyo Blanco this morning, when there are no plants for dyes there?"

Teresita bowed her head for a moment. Then she turned to Josefina and cupped Josefina's cheek in her hand. "I will not tell you," she said. "I cannot."

Josefina was disappointed, but she made herself ask another question. "At the stream, I heard someone whistling the tune of your lullaby," she said. "I thought it was Don Javier, but now I'm not so sure. Do you have any idea who the whistler might have been?"

"A whistler?" said Teresita. "We Navajo are taught, 'Don't whistle too loud, or you will call up the wind.'" Teresita added, "It's serious to summon the wind. The wind is powerful. It is the source of life and breath."

"I don't know who or what the whistler was summoning," said Josefina. "I guess what I'm asking is, was it *you*? Was the whistler someone who had come to meet you? I—"

But Teresita interrupted her. "Stop, dear child," she said. "You must not question me. You must *trust* me." Tenderly, she stroked Josefina's cheek, and then she turned away and went back to her weaving.

With a heavy heart and a mind beset by doubts and even more questions than before, Josefina left, struggling against a feeling of defeat.

"How thoughtful of you, Josefina," said Tía Dolores.

It was after dinner, and Josefina was serving sagebrush tea in the family sala. Taking great care

to keep her hands steady, Josefina poured first Tía
Dolores and then everyone else a cup of hot, aro-
matic tea. Steam arose from their cups, filling the
room with the spicy scent of sagebrush and, because
Josefina had sweetened the tea, the sunny, summery
scent of honey.

Tía Dolores took a sip, and sighed. "Ah, it's so
delicious, and the warmth is sinking into my very
bones. Thank you, Josefina."

"Sí," yawned Papá. "This tea is soothing. We'll all
sleep well and soundly tonight."

Josefina sipped her tea. She silently thanked her
Tía Magdalena for teaching her how to make the
tea, which was so blessedly helping Tía Dolores feel
better. Tía Dolores's face had not looked so serene
in a while. *Not since the night Don Javier gave her the
Glowing Heart ring,* thought Josefina. Oh, if only there
were a tea to soothe doubts such as the ones Josefina
had about Teresita! If only there were a potion to
give Josefina the power to solve the mystery of the

disappearance of the ring, and to frighten any thieves or raiders away!

"I'll make another pot of sagebrush tea tomorrow," she promised Tía Dolores. "And every day, if you wish."

"What a blessing you are, dear Josefina!" said Tía Dolores. She took another sip of tea, her eyes smiling lovingly at Josefina over the rim of the teacup.

chapter 7

Lucita

A LIGHT, LACY dusting of icy snow sparkled in the light of the rising sun as Josefina went to the stream to fill a water jar for Carmen, as she did every morning at sunup. She was up a bit earlier than usual today. Despite the tea, she had had a restless night, imagining that she heard creaks and thumps and doors opening and closing somewhere in the house. Of course, the sounds must have been caused by the wind that had blown in the frosty mix of sleet and snow during the night, and then later blown the clouds away. The ground had a sugary crust now, and the tree branches, coated with ice, glittered like crystal. Josefina felt as if she were walking in an enchanted forest made of silver and glass. A thin layer of ice covered the water at the edge of the stream, caught between the rocks. Josefina was sorry to break the delicate ice when she pushed the heavy water jar through it to get to the water below.

Josefina sang softly to herself as she crouched, waiting for the jar to fill. Suddenly, the icy bushes rattled. Josefina tensed. A large animal crashed through the bushes, thundering down toward Josefina, and—*Oh!* Josefina gasped in surprise. The animal was Lucita, Señor Fernando's portly mule. Lucita was dragging her reins behind her. The thick rope she carried had come uncoiled, and her bulging saddlebags bounced and clanked against her sides.

"Lucita? Where did you come from?" Josefina asked. She grabbed the mule's reins.

"Lucita!" came a cry. Señor Fernando blundered his way through the bushes. When he saw Josefina, he stopped short, startled. "My dear Señorita Montoya!" Señor Fernando said in surprise. "How lovely to see you! What are *you* doing here?"

Josefina was puzzled. She wished she could ask Señor Fernando the same question he had asked her: Why was he here? Had he been to Los Cerrillos and back already? Josefina stood and bowed her head, as she had been taught to do when speaking to an adult. "Con permiso, señor," she said. "I fetch water from the stream for the kitchen every morning at sunrise. In fact, I was here twice yesterday. Did I see you here, as well, a little later than this?"

"No, no, little señorita," said Señor Fernando. "I have only now returned from Los Cerrillos."

Did he travel all night? Josefina wondered. *That's odd.* But she said, "Permit me to lead you to the house. I know my father will be glad to see you."

"How kind of you!" said Señor Fernando. As Josefina handed Lucita's reins to Señor Fernando, he smiled and said, "My mule seems to think of you as a friend."

"I fed her some dried apple once," said Josefina,

"and scratched her nose and sang to her."

"Ah! That's why she rushed down here to the stream," said Señor Fernando. "She must have heard you singing, though I did not. Mules hear better than men!" He laughed. "Well, Lucita is thirsty, and I am dirty, so she shall drink and I shall wash off a bit."

Josefina noticed that he looked a good deal dirtier than travelers usually did, especially considering the fact that the road had a thin covering of snow, so it was not as dusty as usual. Señor Fernando's coat was streaked with dirt, his shirt was untucked and rumpled, and his bright red sash, which previously cinched his trim waist so proudly, was ragged and torn. As he knelt to wash, Josefina turned away and stooped to lift the water jar onto her shoulder. Out of the corner of her eye, she saw Señor Fernando get up. Moving swiftly, he slipped Lucita's saddlebags off and tucked them under a rotten log. *Ah, Señor Fernando wants to relieve Lucita of her burden for a while,*

Josefina thought. The saddlebags did look heavier and more bulgy than before. Josefina hid a smile, thinking: *Señor Fernando is so proper and polite, most likely he has brought gifts for all of us from Los Cerrillos, and wants to surprise us with them later. If so, Clara will be more impressed than ever with his good manners, and Antonio will be more convinced than ever that he is one of the three kings!* Josefina's own good manners prevented her from saying anything. She knew that it was not her place as a child to question what any adult did, especially one that was so honored a guest of her Papá's as Señor Fernando. She stood and lifted her water jar onto her shoulder.

"There!" said Señor Fernando as he dried his hands on the ends of his sash. "That's better."

Papá, Tía Dolores, and Josefina's sisters were on their way to morning prayers when Josefina led Señor Fernando to them in the courtyard. "Perdón, Papá," said Josefina. "Señor Fernando is here. I found him and his mule Lucita down by the stream."

"Ah, indeed," said Papá. If they thought it was odd that Señor Fernando had made the journey from Los Cerrillos at night, both Papá and Tía Dolores were far too polite to question him about it. Papá said only, "Welcome back, señor. You were at the stream? Were you lost? Perhaps you rode past the house by mistake."

"Gracias, Señor Montoya. You are kindness itself," said Señor Fernando. "But no, no, I was not lost. I went to the stream to let my mule Lucita drink and to wash myself up a bit."

He did? Josefina thought. She'd had the impression that Lucita had broken away from Señor Fernando. She must have been wrong, because Señor Fernando went on to explain: "I thought it would be boorish and disrespectful of me to appear before you or your lovely wife with the dust of the road upon me while conducting the business of buying your horse."

Papá bowed. "Your considerate manners are a model for us all," he said.

"Ah, but I have interrupted your morning," said Señor Fernando to Tía Dolores. His face collapsed into sorrowful concern. "I must ask you to forgive me. Beautiful ladies such as yourself are delicate flowers, and I know you need quiet, restful mornings. You're not like us rough and ready men."

Tía Dolores hid a smile. Josefina knew that she did not consider herself a "delicate flower." Tía Dolores's energy usually put them all to shame, even Papá. It was only because she was feeling unwell that she was quieter than usual. "Señor Fernando, you must join us for morning prayers, and then breakfast," said Tía Dolores.

"Oh, no, señora!" protested Señor Fernando, polite as ever. "I could not possibly intrude upon you in such a way! No, no." He turned to Papá. "If it suits you, sir, I will join you for prayers, and then you and I will conclude our business and I will be on my way with Valiente and leave you to enjoy your breakfast in peace."

"As you wish," said Papá.

After prayers Papá said, "Josefina, please go
to the stable and ask Miguel for a halter and rope.
Señor Fernando and I will go to the pasture and
lead Valiente back here to the house. Then we can
conclude our business, and Señor Fernando can take
Valiente back to Los Cerrillos."

"Sí, Papá," said Josefina. She was always glad
to be able to help Papá. Quickly, Josefina ran to the
stable and gave Miguel Papá's instructions. Miguel
allowed her to carry the halter and rope. Josefina
slung them over her shoulder under her sarape, and
she and Miguel followed the path that Papá and
Señor Fernando, leading his mule Lucita, had taken
up to the fenced pasture where Valiente was kept
during the winter months. Because there was scant
grass for grazing, Miguel hauled hay and water to
the pasture for Valiente every day.

Josefina pulled her sarape over her head and
held it close to protect herself against the cruel cold.

Fast-moving clouds scudded over the mountain, blocking the sun and casting shadows below.

When Miguel and Josefina got to the pasture, Papá turned to them with a concerned frown. "Valiente is not here," he said. "Miguel, did you move him?"

"No, señor," answered Miguel. "I brought Valiente his hay and water here before dark yesterday. Do you think Valiente has been stolen?"

"Stolen? The saints preserve us!" exclaimed Señor Fernando, sounding alarmed. "This is terribly distressing. I must say, I did not expect such a delay, and—"

"Calm yourself, señor," Papá interrupted. He took a moment to calm himself, too, and then he said, "I'll question all my workers to see if someone else moved the horse, and I'll send out a search party, as well." Josefina heard the resolve and the controlled force in his voice as he went on. "The horse may have jumped the fence and wandered off on his own. In any case, I promise you that we'll find Valiente whether he's been moved, run off, or stolen. I'll offer a handsome reward for finding the horse."

"Excelente," said Señor Fernando. "Very wise. Of course, I want to be of help. I too will search for the horse. I will begin immediately."

"Surely not," said Papá. "You can't search on an empty stomach. Take Lucita to the stable, and then join us for breakfast. After we've eaten, you and I can search together."

"Very well," said Señor Fernando, though Josefina could tell that he was impatient to begin searching. He led Lucita to the stable as Papá and Josefina headed toward the house.

Josefina knew that Papá was deeply worried about Valiente. She slipped her hand into Papá's to comfort him, but he squeezed her hand only distractedly in reply. Josefina glanced up at Papá. Oh, how she wanted to help him! Perhaps the man she had heard whistling the lullaby at the stream was a horse thief. She must tell Papá. Josefina knew that it was not a child's place to begin a conversation with an adult, but this was an extraordinary circumstance. So, with polite respect, she said, "Papá?"

"Sí, *niña*?" he answered.

"Yesterday I was scrubbing a pan at the stream," she said, "and I heard a man whistling Teresita's lullaby. I thought it must be Don Javier. But when I called out to him, he didn't answer, and all I saw was a flash of red flying off in the direction of Arroyo Blanco." Josefina silently asked God to forgive her for not telling Papá about the thread of red wool she'd found caught on the branch in Arroyo Blanco. That thread might have been from Teresita's blanket, and despite Teresita's refusal to answer Josefina's questions, Josefina still couldn't bear to hint that Teresita was involved in any wrongdoing. "Maybe the man I heard at the stream could be a horse thief who stole Valiente."

Papá stopped. He turned to Josefina and took

both her hands in his own. "Miguel told me that
you thought you saw a man on the way home from
Santiago's house," he said. "Did you see the same
man at the stream?"

Josefina shook her head apologetically. "I didn't
see either one very well," she said. "So I don't
know."

Papá sighed. "I don't know either," he said ear-
nestly. "But I *do* know that this is no business for a
young girl like you to be involved in. I couldn't bear
it if anything harmed you, Josefina. You're growing
up now, but you're still my little bird, and you must
promise me to fly far away from danger."

"I promise," said Josefina. She stood up straight
so that she wouldn't look like such a *very* little bird
or, at least, she'd be one that had strong wings.

Back at the house, the whole family sat down
to a very rushed and strained meal. Even Señor
Fernando was quiet. He focused hard on his breakfast, concentrating his usual intense energy on

eating and drinking as much as he could, rather than talking. Only Antonio managed to eat as much breakfast as Señor Fernando did: Josefina and her sisters were upset to see Papá perplexed and disappointed and Tía Dolores distressed.

After breakfast, Antonio went to the stable to do his morning chores for Miguel, and Señor Fernando and Papá left to go look for Valiente. Tía Dolores gave Clara the little key to the locked compartment in the cupboard, because there was the silver tray to polish and put away, left over from the fancy midday meal they'd had for Señor Fernando. Then Tía Dolores excused herself, looking ill, so the sisters set to work tidying up the family sala and washing the dishes without her.

Francisca was as tight-lipped and grumpy as she always was when doing chores, except when she polished the silver tray, because she could admire her reflection in it as if it were a mirror.

"That's enough," said Clara bossily. She took her

hands out of the dishwater, dried them, and then took the tray away from Francisca. "You'll make it all cloudy by breathing on it." She gave the silver tray and Tía Dolores's little key to Josefina. "Please put the tray away, Josefina," she said, and then she went back to washing the dishes.

Josefina trotted off to the family sala with the tray and the key. She reached up and opened the cupboard. When she did, she saw that she didn't need the key after all; the little door to the interior compartment was unlocked, and cracked a bit ajar. *That's odd,* she thought. As she stood on her tiptoes to open the little door all the way in order to put the tray inside, she made a terrible discovery. The compartment was empty. The rest of the silver was gone.

Her heart beating wildly, Josefina ran back to the kitchen. "The silver compartment is empty!" she said. "The silver is gone. It's all gone."

"Oh, no!" moaned Francisca. "Gone? You mean

stolen! Just like the ring, the empanadas, and Valiente. Someone has stolen our silver."

"But how?" asked Clara, lifting her dripping hands palms up from the dishwater. "Who could have sneaked into the house past the guards?"

"I don't know," said Francisca. "Maybe it was stolen by someone who was already inside the house."

"Do you mean a servant?" asked Clara.

"I don't *know*," said Francisca again. "But I do know that we had better tell Papá about the theft right away."

"We can't," said Clara. "He and Señor Fernando have left to go look for Valiente."

"And we mustn't go bothering Tía Dolores," said Josefina. "She's ill. We'll just have to wait until Papá gets back before we give him the bad news."

"Oh!" Clara exploded. She plunked a big bowl flat into the tub so that the soapy water splashed up, making Josefina and Francisca jump. "Lately there's nothing *but* bad news around here, and it's all the fault of that ring. Nothing has been right since Don Javier brought it here. I wish he had never given it to Tía Dolores!"

"Maybe he wishes that, too," said Francisca.

"What do you mean?" asked Josefina.

Francisca leaned forward conspiratorially. "We discovered that the Glowing Heart ring had disappeared just after Don Javier supposedly left for Cordero, didn't we?" she said. "Maybe he stole the ring back, and then later, stole the horse and the silver, too, out of jealousy that Papá is married to Tía Dolores." She sighed sentimentally. "He stole from Papá because Papá stole his one true love from him."

"For heaven's sake! You goose!" said Clara. "If Don Javier stole anything, he did it because he needed the money. Didn't we all hear him say that he couldn't buy Papá's horse, and that he knew what it was to part with a priceless treasure? I think he meant the ring was the treasure, and he stole it and the horse and the silver to sell them for money."

"Stop, both of you," said Josefina, trying to make peace. "It's wicked to accuse Don Javier of being a thief for love *or* money. We shouldn't think ill of him just because we're afraid he makes Tía Dolores discontent with life on the rancho. Besides, why would he come all the way to Santa Fe to give Tía Dolores the ring, only to steal it back?"

"Well, Abuelito *told* him to bring it," said Clara. "And if you didn't want to be suspected of stealing it, wouldn't you make a big showy presentation of delivering it, just as that trickster Don Javier did? Someone who makes things appear as if by magic can make things disappear, too. And hasn't he disappeared himself? He may be halfway to Mexico City now, for all we know!"

"Perhaps . . . or perhaps not," said Josefina slowly. "At the stream yesterday I heard a man whistling Teresita's lullaby—the tune that Don Javier likes so much."

"That settles it!" said Francisca. "Don Javier took the ring when he and Tía Dolores were in the kitchen, when she was packing food for his trip. Then he just pretended to go to Cordero. Really, he's been hiding nearby. He took the overcooked empanadas, and now he has stolen Valiente and the silver, too."

"I saw a flash of red at the stream, which could have been Don Javier's scarf," said Josefina. "Or, well, also . . . When I went to Santiago's hut, I thought I saw someone watching us, and *he* was wearing red, too."

"A stranger!" breathed Francisca. Then, looking at Clara out of the corner of her eye, she taunted, "Of course, Señor Fernando wears a red sash, too."

"And he knows the tune to the lullaby, because he heard Don Javier whistling it and Tía Dolores playing it on the piano the first day he came to the rancho," said Josefina. "Maybe *he's* the culprit."

"No!" Clara exclaimed, exasperated. Then she went on, with impressive logic, "It doesn't make sense. If Señor Fernando stole Valiente, why would he have returned this morning? Why wouldn't he have just ridden off on Valiente in the night, leading Lucita behind him? And use your heads: No one from outside the household could have stolen the silver. As I asked before, how could anyone have sneaked into the house and stolen it without being seen by the guard? Really, the very idea of Señor Fernando stealing a horse and silver is ridiculous. Why, he is the most elegant, correct, and polite gentleman I've ever met! Such exquisite manners! Have you ever seen a more proper person?"

"No," Josefina admitted. "It's just that, well, sometimes his praise is so exaggerated that I wonder if he is entirely sincere." She thought for a moment and then said, "Clara, remember how you said that Don Javier isn't sensible or serious, and doesn't *say* what he *means*? Well, I think sometimes Señor Fernando doesn't *mean* what he *says*. And if he hasn't been honest with us, then maybe he hasn't been honest in his dealings with Papá, either. Maybe he *has* been sneaking around. If it wasn't Don Javier and it wasn't a stranger, maybe I *did* see Señor Fernando rushing away from the stream when I was scrubbing the pan after I burned the empanadas."

Francisca, who was shamelessly irreverent even in solemn situations, pretended to be Señor Fernando. "Beautiful young lady," she said to Josefina, "it is poor manners for me to contradict you, but I must tell you that you are mistaken. I never rush. That would be unseemly."

"How can you joke at a time like this?" Clara scolded Francisca. "You are even less sensible and serious than that sneak Don Javier!"

But Francisca ignored Clara. "I am not a tall fellow, but I always walk with dignity, as befits a respectable man like myself," she said. "My mule Lucita is not fast, either, because though I love to eat empanadas, it is *Lucita* who is stout, not I."

"Poor Lucita!" said Josefina. "I feel sorry for her."

"Stop!" Clara interrupted. "Stop this foolishness! Thievery is not a joking matter."

At last, Francisca became serious. In her own voice, she said, "I think whoever Josefina heard whistling at the stream must be the thief who stole the ring, the empanadas, and now, Valiente and the silver. The question is, *who*? Is it Don Javier, Señor Fernando, or a dangerous stranger?"

Josefina turned away. She did not want to say anything to stir up questions in her sisters' minds about one more person who might be involved somehow: Teresita. Josefina didn't want to tell her sisters about the piece of red wool that she had found, or Teresita's refusal to explain why she had gone to Arroyo Blanco. Francisca and Clara were sure to catch the contagion of suspicion. They'd quickly realize that Teresita knew about the ring, and that she would not have had to break in to the house to steal the silver—she needed only the little key. Then they might think that Teresita had stolen Valiente to get away.

Josefina took a deep breath. The best way to prove that Teresita was *not* the thief was to prove who *was*. Josefina was determined to find out. Clara was right: The thievery that was plaguing her family was serious, and it had to *stop*.

chapter 8
The Wind

AS SOON AS the dishes were done, Josefina went
to find Miguel. He and Antonio were in the stable.
Miguel was getting a halter and a rope.

"Your papá and Señor Fernando left together to
go look for Valiente," said Antonio. "And now Miguel
is leaving to look for Valiente, too."

"Where will you be going to look?" Josefina asked
Miguel.

"I'm going to Arroyo Verde," said Miguel. "I think
Valiente was stolen. But there's a chance that he
jumped the fence and ran away. If so, there's water
in the stream that runs through Arroyo Verde, and
Valiente may have smelled it and gone there to drink."

"May I come with you?" asked Josefina. "I'd like
to help you."

"No, dear child," said Miguel. He sounded like
Papá when he said, "Looking for a horse that's run off
or been stolen is no job for you."

Josefina thought fast. She was determined to go
to the arroyo to help look for Valiente and, she hoped,
find clues about the thief so that she could prove
Teresita's innocence to herself and everyone else, if
necessary. "Ah," she said, "but I want to go to Arroyo
Verde. I need to find more sagebrush leaves. The tea
I made seemed to help Tía Dolores feel better, at least
for a little while, last night."

"Very well," said Miguel. She had known that
he would; *everyone* wanted to help Tía Dolores feel
better. And anyway, it was partly true: She *did* intend
to look for sagebrush leaves.

"I'm good at finding things, and I like horses,"
said Antonio. "Can I come, too?"

"No," said Josefina. "Not this time."

Antonio's face was so flooded with disappointment that Josefina felt sorry for him.

"But you know," she said solemnly, "someone must do an important job right here in the stable. Lots of times, a horse that's been lost or stolen finds its *own* way home. Can you remember to look out the stable window from time to time, to see if Valiente has come home by himself?"

"Yes!" said Antonio proudly. Immediately, he turned over a wooden bucket, stood on it, and took up his post looking out the stable window. He was so small that only his eyes and nose were higher than the sill, but he looked determined to be of help.

"Come along, then, señorita," Miguel said. "It's not far to Arroyo Verde, but we had best be going. If Valiente has wandered off, the sooner we follow him the better."

Miguel led the way. They headed east. Josefina walked as fast as she could so as not to slow down Miguel. In a short while, Miguel and Josefina had arrived at the edge of Arroyo Verde. A narrow trickle of a stream zigzagged sharply back and forth as it knifed its way through the arroyo, winding, twisting, turning, doubling back on itself, and cutting little caverns into the rock and dirt sides.

Suddenly, Miguel stopped. He pointed. Josefina looked, and gasped. There, in one of the gullies between two sharp turns, was Papá's precious horse, Valiente. And not only that, but Valiente was being petted by a tall, strange man wearing a fringed blanket. Josefina squinted to see the man better. He looked Indian. It was odd; she felt as though she had seen him before. *He's the shadow man I saw on the mountain,* she realized in a burst of recognition. *I was not imagining him. He is real, as real as his blanket with the red fringe on it. And here he is, with Valiente. That tall man must be the horse thief! Surely, he took the ring and the silver, too.* Josefina's heart lifted. If this man was the thief, then Don Javier, Señor Fernando, and best of all, Teresita, were all innocent.

Miguel held his finger to his lips to signal Josefina

to be silent. Stealthily, they sank down, crouching behind a clump of *piñón*.

In a desperate whisper, Josefina said to Miguel, "*That's* the man I saw on the mountain when we were coming home from Santiago's hut! He's a thief! He has stolen Valiente!"

"The scoundrel!" gasped Miguel. Then he whispered to Josefina, "That man is dangerous. You must stay safely up here, at the top of the arroyo. Stay quiet and stay hidden. I'm going to climb down and confront him."

Josefina nodded. Without a sound, she followed Miguel to the edge of the arroyo, crawling forward on her hands and knees. She lay down on her stomach to watch him climb down to the bottom. Miguel was only partway down when Josefina saw *another* man come out from the shadow cast by the opposite side of the arroyo. The last part of the path was treacherously steep and rocky, so he was leading his mule rather than riding it.

With a shock, Josefina realized that the mule was Lucita and the man was Señor Fernando! *He must have made a lucky guess, and come straight to Arroyo Verde to look for Valiente,* Josefina reasoned. *But where is Papá?*

There was a commotion down in the arroyo. Startled by the sight of Señor Fernando and Lucita, Valiente reared up, whinnying wildly. Frightened Lucita brayed, jerked her head, ripped her reins out of Señor Fernando's hands, and backed away, still braying.

"What are you doing with that horse?" Señor Fernando shouted to the tall man. "Get away from that horse!"

Josefina rose up on her elbows. Señor Fernando didn't sound at all like his usual dignified, polite self. Josefina was going to call out to him, but Miguel had told her to stay silent and hidden, so she did as she had been told. Señor Fernando growled at the man again, "I told you to get away from that horse!"

He waved his arms angrily as he stormed across the little stream.

The tall man stood frowning defiantly, unafraid of Señor Fernando, and unafraid of rearing, bucking Valiente. Josefina was not surprised that Valiente was acting wild; Lucita's braying had upset the high-strung horse. Though the tall man didn't seem to understand the Spanish words that Señor Fernando was shouting at him, he clearly understood the anger in the words. As Señor Fernando walked toward him, the man spoke in an unfamiliar language and held up his hand to stop Señor Fernando. But Señor Fernando bravely barreled toward him, still shouting and gesticulating. Neither man saw Miguel, or heard him call out. Then Señor Fernando shoved the tall man hard, so hard that he fell and hit his head on a rock. He lay unmoving. *Is he unconscious,* Josefina wondered, *or is he dead?*

She could hardly breathe as she saw Miguel, now at the bottom of the canyon, approach Señor

Fernando. "Señor!" Miguel called out again.

This time, Señor Fernando heard. He spun around quickly, and looked fearful until he recognized Miguel. "Look!" he said to Miguel. "I found Valiente. *And* I found the thief who stole him, too!"

"Well done, señor," said Miguel. "Where is Señor Montoya?"

"I don't know. We started out searching together," said Señor Fernando, "but I said that we'd cover more territory and find Valiente quicker if we split up. As you can see, I was right."

"Sí!" agreed Miguel.

"I've knocked the thief unconscious," said Señor Fernando. "But he's much bigger than I am, and when he wakes up, he'll be too much even for the two of us to handle along with that skittish horse Valiente. We'll need help. I'll stay here and you go get Señor Montoya so that he can help us bring the thief and the horse back to the rancho. Lucita allows only me to ride her, so you'll have to walk."

"Very well, señor," said Miguel. He handed Señor Fernando the halter and climbed out of the arroyo. As he passed Josefina, he signaled to her, so she stood and followed him.

"We'll have to walk quickly," said Miguel. "It will take us a quarter of an hour to get back to the rancho. Will you be all right?"

"Sí," said Josefina firmly.

But in fact, they had walked only a minute or two when Papá rode up on a spotted horse.

"Señor Fernando has found your horse and the thief in Arroyo Verde," said Miguel.

"Thanks be to God," said Papá. He slid off his spotted horse, and Miguel and Josefina led him to the arroyo. Papá's horse had to pick its way slowly down the narrow path to the bottom, so as Josefina followed it, she had plenty of time to see that Señor Fernando had tied the hands of the tall man with a rope, even though the man was still unconscious. Now Señor Fernando was struggling to put Miguel's halter on Valiente. But the powerful horse kicked and bucked and shied away so that Señor Fernando could not slip the halter over its head.

"Steady! Stand still, you wild creature," ordered Señor Fernando. Though he spoke in his most commanding tone, the frightened horse would not obey. It wouldn't even allow him to come close.

Papá called out, "Señor Fernando!"

Señor Fernando jumped, and then turned to face Papá. He smiled, and when he spoke, he poured out gratitude. "Oh, thank goodness you are here already, my dear friend Señor Montoya!" he exclaimed. "I see that your servant found you." Señor Fernando looked confused when he spotted Josefina, but quickly turned his attention back to Papá. He held out the halter to him and said, "You'll be able to control Valiente. I cannot. I think Lucita has frightened him."

Papá pointed to the tall man. "What about this man?" he asked.

"That man is the thief who stole your horse!" said Señor Fernando. "Stay away from him. I've tied his hands, and he is unconscious, but when he wakes up, he'll be dangerous. He tried to attack me!"

Josefina was perplexed. She thought she'd seen Señor Fernando attack the thief, and not the other way around. *I must have been too far away to see what was really happening,* she thought. *How brave of small, slight Señor Fernando to fight the thief who looks so tall and strong!*

As Papá and Miguel put the halter on Valiente and Señor Fernando took Lucita's reins, Josefina looked at the man lying on the ground. She expected to feel scared of him, but somehow, she didn't. In fact, she felt sorry for him. Even if he was a horse thief, her kind heart hated to see him suffer and her instincts as a young curandera compelled her to help him.

Swiftly, quietly, Josefina took off her sash and dampened it in the tiny stream, and softly, gently, she used it to wipe the man's brow. The man stirred and groaned. To reassure him, Josefina spoke the few words she knew in the language her Pueblo friends spoke, but the words seemed to have no effect and the poor man groaned in pain and distress again. Josefina wished that she could find some way to help him rest more comfortably. Thinking of Teresita, and how her singing always calmed Antonio, Josefina began to sing Teresita's lullaby:

> She'awéé' ałts'ísí t'áadoo nichaaí, t'áadoo nichaaí.
> Hazhó'ígo iłhosh,
> Hazhó'ígo iłhosh k'ad,
> Hazhó'ígo iłhosh.

With a sigh, the man opened his eyes.

Ah, thought Josefina. *He understands! He must know some words in Navajo!*

The man smiled up at her and said only one word: "Josefina." Then he closed his eyes and sank back into unconsciousness.

Josefina's heart stood still. *How did the man know her name?*

By now, Papá and Miguel had put the halter on Valiente, who stood calmly, though he did tense when he saw Señor Fernando and Lucita come toward him.

"Whoa, there, Valiente," Papá said softly. Once again the horse quieted. Papá lifted the unconscious man onto the spotted horse behind Miguel. As he did so, the man came to. He tried to talk, frowning and nodding his head toward Señor Fernando, but no one could understand him.

Señor Fernando frowned at him. "Save your breath, you deceitful thief!" he said. Papá mounted Valiente and lifted Josefina up to sit in front of him, and they all rode back to the rancho, Señor Fernando riding a tired Lucita at the end of the line.

With Papá's arms around her, Josefina felt safe and steady even high atop huge Valiente. But her mind was in a whirl. *How did the man know her name?*

Why had he smiled at her? If he was the man she had seen on the mountain, what was he doing at Arroyo Verde? Was he a good man, or was he what Señor Fernando had called him: a deceitful thief?

chapter 9

The Truth

"COCK-A-DOODLE-DOO," Francisca murmured into Josefina's ear. "Listen to the rooster, crowing over his bravery." She rolled her eyes toward Señor Fernando.

"I feared for my life," he was saying, "as that tall man hurled himself at me. He had stolen the horse, and now he was attacking me." Almost every member of the household was gathered in the storeroom. Because its door could be locked, Papá and Miguel had chosen the storeroom as the best place to keep the accused thief until the authorities could come. Everyone listened intently as Señor Fernando told his tale. "But then I said to myself, 'I cannot let this ruffian get away with stealing the horse of my esteemed friend, Señor Montoya.' So, without a thought for my own safety, I pushed the thief down with such force that he struck his head and fell into unconsciousness."

"Ah!" said everyone.

Señor Fernando's eyes were bright as he turned to Papá. "I no longer wish to buy your horse," he said. "Valiente is too spirited for me, and he doesn't like Lucita. But in truth, in all modesty, I do believe I have earned the reward for finding Valiente for you. I even apprehended the thief who stole him."

Papá bowed. "I am grateful for your help," he began.

But at that moment, the accused thief cried out. He seemed to be trying urgently to explain something to them all, frustrated by the fact that no one understood him.

"Quiet, you," said Señor Fernando. He turned to Papá. "We all know the bad deeds this man has done. Nothing he could say will change our minds. We're sure he's the thief."

But Josefina was *not* sure. Something nagged at her. She kept remembering the moment when the

man had smiled at her and said her name. He hadn't
looked at all like a bad man or a thief then. If he
looked desperate now, it was no wonder. His hands
were bound, he was soon to be locked up, and he
kept trying to talk but no one understood him.
Anyone would be desperate in that situation.

Josefina tugged on Tía Dolores's sleeve. "Shouldn't
the tall man have a chance to speak for himself?" she
asked her stepmother.

Tía Dolores nodded. Her face was pale, but her
voice was clear and firm as she spoke Josefina's
question aloud, "Surely the accused thief deserves
a chance to speak for himself and be understood?"

Señor Fernando bowed low, and in his regal
manner, he said to Tía Dolores, "Ah, my dear, beautiful señora! As all women do, you're letting your
heart rule your head. It would be a waste of precious
time to listen to the man. He's a thief and a liar. It's
clear that he's guilty. In any case, your idea is impossible." He shrugged and held his hands out palms up

in a gesture of helplessness. "The thief can't speak Spanish. No one here speaks whatever language it is that he speaks. If we spoke to him, he wouldn't understand one word."

He understood the words to the Navajo lullaby, thought Josefina. *Maybe he speaks Navajo!* At that moment, Josefina knew what to do. Swiftly, as silently as a shadow, she slipped out of the storeroom and ran to the kitchen, where Carmen, Teresita, and Antonio were making empanadas. "Please, Teresita," she said, "come with me."

"Can I come?" asked Antonio, as usual.

"Not right now," said Josefina apologetically. She took Teresita by the hand, and in no time they were back in the storeroom. Teresita gasped, but then stood tall at her side.

"What's this? What's this?" huffed Señor Fernando when he saw them.

But Josefina ignored him. She gathered all her courage and spoke directly to Papá. "Forgive me,

Papá," she said. She was out of breath from running and she was trembling at her own boldness. "The man understood the words to Teresita's lullaby, so I think he speaks Navajo."

"And he is wearing a Navajo blanket," said Tía Dolores, "so I think he *is* Navajo."

"He's a thief!" burst out Señor Fernando. "He probably stole that blanket!"

But Josefina refused to be rattled. She asked Papá, "Will you allow Teresita to translate Navajo into Spanish for the man?"

Papá frowned and folded his arms across his chest. It was *not* proper for a child like Josefina or a servant like Teresita to interfere in such a forward way, especially on behalf of someone accused of stealing his very best horse. But Tía Dolores touched Papá gently on his arm and he nodded. "Very well," he said.

Teresita rushed to the man and sank down by his side. They spoke hurriedly to one another, and then Teresita stood. "This man says that he is not the horse thief. He was in Arroyo Verde yesterday, and he saw Señor Fernando and his mule hiding there. Well before sunrise, Señor Fernando left on foot and then returned in a short while—with Valiente! He tied the horse to a stump and left again on his mule, all before dawn." Teresita nodded toward Señor Fernando. "*He* stole the horse," she said.

"No!" protested Señor Fernando. He looked outraged. "I did no such thing!" He puffed out his chest and said to Papá with offended dignity, "Señor, I know that you will not believe a thieving stranger like that man over a respectable man such as myself. Why, of course you know that I came back today to buy the horse, not to steal it."

Suddenly, Josefina understood: The tall man was telling the truth. She knew that Señor Fernando had lied about the man attacking him first, *and* he had lied about coming to the stream on purpose this morning, too. She also knew that it was rude and bold for her to speak, but she couldn't help it! Mustering all her courage, she faced Señor Fernando. "I think you *did* try to steal Valiente," she blurted out. "When I surprised you at the stream this morning, you lied. You were *not* returning from Los Cerrillos. You were returning from hiding Valiente in the arroyo; that's why you were so dirty. And you lied when you said this man attacked you; I saw you knock him down first. I think that if this man hadn't stopped you, you would've taken Valiente away today. And I think Valiente isn't all that you've tried to steal. I saw you hiding Lucita's saddlebags under the rotten log at the stream this morning. They looked heavy and bulging. Why would you hide them, unless you didn't want anyone to know what's in them?"

"Our missing silver?" gasped Francisca. "And the ring?"

"Our silver is missing?" asked Papá, stunned.

"Sí, Papá," said Francisca, Clara, and Josefina.

"I think it is in Lucita's saddlebags," Josefina

said. "They're at the stream."

At a signal from Papá, Miguel slipped out to go to the stream to look for the saddlebags.

"Where is Miguel going?" barked Señor Fernando. He scowled at Josefina. "How dare you accuse me, you sneaking, spying child!"

He frowned so fiercely at Josefina that she stepped back. Tía Dolores came and stood behind her, supporting her and holding her close by wrapping her arms around her. "Do not speak to my child like that," said Tía Dolores.

"That child—" Señor Fernando began.

But Papá held up his hand. "Quiet, señor," he said. Then he turned to the sisters. "Why didn't you tell me that the silver was missing?"

"You had already left to look for Valiente by the time we discovered it was gone," said Francisca.

"And we didn't want to disturb Tía Dolores," added Clara. "She was resting because she wasn't feeling well."

Papá and Tía Dolores exchanged an anguished look above Josefina's head, but neither spoke.

At this moment, out of breath from running the whole way, Miguel returned. He handed Papá the bulging saddlebags. Papá spilled the contents onto a soft blanket on the floor. Silver spoons fell out, and the sugar bowl and creamer. There were silver candlesticks and small silver dishes, all stolen from the house.

Tía Dolores leaned forward, over Josefina's head, and looked at the heap of silver. Josefina felt her sigh, and understood. The gold-and-ruby Glowing Heart ring was not among the stolen silver.

But the solution to the other mysteries *was*. The stolen silver proved that Señor Fernando was a thief. He had taken Valiente and the silver, which meant that Teresita, Don Javier, and the Navajo man had *not*. Only the theft of the ring was still a mystery. Miguel seized Señor Fernando by one arm and Papá seized the other.

"You played a devious game, Señor Fernando," said Papá. "You pretended to be a respectable horse trader, so we invited you into our home and offered you refreshment."

"You saw me take the silver out of the cupboard in the family sala," said Tía Dolores. "In fact, you *helped* me."

"And then you peppered me with questions about the house," said Papá. "I was flattered, so I answered them all, not realizing that I was help-ing you plan how to break in to rob us. After lunch, you lied, saying that you had to go to Los Cerrillos to get the money to buy Valiente. But really, you hid in Arroyo Verde, and when we were all asleep, you stole Valiente and hid him in the arroyo. Then you sneaked to the house, still before dawn, to steal our silver."

"But how did he get *into* the house?" asked Clara.

"I'm afraid I'm partly to blame for that, too," said Papá ruefully. "When I showed him around, he saw where the lowest part of the wall was. Foolishly, when he asked me to, I explained the guards' rounds to him, so he knew just when and where to throw his rope up and loop it over a rainspout. He must have climbed over the wall and slipped into the family sala."

"That's right," sneered Señor Fernando. "And I can pick any lock—"

"So you didn't need my little key," said Tía Dolores. "It was easy for you to open the compartment, take the silver, and put it in Lucita's saddlebags."

"When Josefina surprised you at the stream you had an alibi: You said you'd returned to buy Valiente," said Papá. "Really, you were on your way back to the arroyo with the stolen silver to get Valiente and ride away forever. If Josefina hadn't seen you, you would have gotten away with it. Why did you decide to stop at the stream?"

"He *didn't* decide to," Josefina answered. "Lucita did. She heard me singing, and she broke away from Señor Fernando, so he had to chase her."

"Lucita likes Josefina, because Josefina fed her," Clara piped up, carried away with excitement.

"When Josefina saw you, you realized that you'd have to hide the silver and come up to the house and pretend to buy Valiente," said Papá to Señor Fernando. "And you still might have been able to get away with Valiente if this Navajo man hadn't been in the arroyo."

"And you might have convinced my husband to give you the reward money, if it weren't for Josefina," said Tía Dolores. "She was smart enough to think of finding someone to translate Navajo into Spanish."

Papá smiled at Josefina. "Yes," he said. "My Josefina *is* smart, isn't she?"

Josefina smiled back at Papá. Never had she felt more proud.

Later, the authorities came to take Señor Fernando away to await trial. Papá untied the Navajo man's hands and, after an intense conversation with Teresita, the Navajo man was about to leave, too, but Papá stopped him.

"Teresita," said Papá sternly. "I'm grateful to this man for helping us catch Señor Fernando. But he may be a troublemaker, too. Ask him what his name is, and where he is from, and why he has been lurking near my rancho."

Teresita spoke to the man in Navajo, and much to everyone's surprise, she and the man smiled. Teresita put her arm around the man's shoulders and said, "I don't need to ask him. I know who he is. This man is my brother, Níyol, whom I have not seen for many, many years."

"What?" everyone gasped.

Josefina ran to Teresita and flung her arms around her. She was so happy! Now everything made sense. Níyol was Teresita's secret. She really had been meeting someone: *her brother*! Teresita was completely innocent of any wrongdoing, and had been all along.

"Oh, Teresita," said Tía Dolores. "You must have been so happy to see your brother Níyol again."

"Sí," said Teresita. "Níyol was hunting in the mountains the day that Josefina, Miguel, and I went to Santiago's hut. When he heard me singing the Navajo lullaby that he knew so well from our childhood, he began to follow us. When I went outside to fasten the bundle of wool onto our mule, he spoke to me. That was a blessed moment! We hadn't seen each other since we were parted as children years ago. We couldn't speak long. But he followed us from a distance as we made our way home. Once, he came so close that Josefina saw him, so he hid again."

"There's a great deal of ill feeling between the Navajos and the Spanish farmers," said Papá, frowning and crossing his arms over his chest. "We don't trust each other. I'm sure that's why your brother didn't want to reveal himself."

Teresita nodded in agreement. "Níyol thought it would cause trouble," she said. "You might think that

I was planning to run off with him, or that he was lurking around the rancho looking for stock to steal. So Níyol and I both thought it was best to keep him a secret. Most of the time, Níyol stayed safely hidden, and I brought food to him. One day, I looked for him in Arroyo Blanco, but I couldn't find him. So I left, and met him on my way home. It turned out that he had ventured all the way to the stream to warn me because he had seen Señor Fernando acting suspiciously—"

"That's when I heard Níyol whistling the lullaby," said Josefina, "and saw just a flash of the red on his blanket before he disappeared."

"Yes. Remember? I told you that his name, Níyol, means 'wind,' and it suits him!" said Teresita. "He's had to be as quick and as invisible as the wind so he wouldn't be spotted. On the day Níyol came to the stream, he thought you were me, Josefina. You answered the whistle, and that was the signal we'd agreed upon to find each other for our meetings. That was the day you saw me returning from Arroyo

Blanco. The red wool you saw caught on a branch was from the fringe of my blanket. I am sorry that I couldn't answer the questions you asked me about that day, but I had to protect my brother."

"Of course!" said Josefina with all her heart. "I'm glad you did."

Níyol smiled and said something to Teresita. She explained, "My brother wants me to tell you that during our meetings, I told him that I am respected and well treated by your family, and that Josefina, Clara, Francisca, Ana, Juan, and Antonio are the children of my heart now."

Níyol said something more, something that made Teresita smile as she explained, "I brought Níyol my own meals to eat, and I told him that it was you, Josefina, the girl he saw with me on the mountain, who had made the less-than-perfect empanadas I brought to him as well."

"So *that's* where they disappeared to!" said Josefina.

"Yes, and that's how Níyol knew your name," said Teresita, "and that's why he smiled at you when you sang to him and washed his brow. He already thought of you as a friend."

"*Shik'is*," said Níyol to Josefina.

"*Shik'is*," she said in reply. Josefina did not need Teresita to translate for her. She knew that *shik'is* meant "my friend."

chapter 10

Hearts Aglow

EVERYONE WAS SORRY when Níyol left
the next day. Teresita gave him a beautiful woven
blanket to remember her by. Josefina helped Carmen
pack food for Níyol—including plenty of empanadas—to take on his way. And Papá gave him two
sheep as a reward.

As they waved good-bye, Josefina said to
Francisca, "I'm glad Papá gave Níyol a reward.
He deserves it. He really was the one who found
Valiente."

"Níyol is the answer to where the missing food
went, too," said Francisca. "Now the only mystery
that remains is . . ." Her sentence ended in a sigh.
Josefina understood: They all felt discouraged. It
seemed as though Tía Dolores's golden Glowing

Heart ring was lost forever.

"We may never know what happened to Tía Dolores's ring," said Clara. "But it seems that Señor Fernando told the truth about one thing: He didn't steal it. I suppose there's still the chance that Don Javier took the ring and ran off to Mexico City with it. Such mischief would be just like him."

The girls went inside, washed their hands, and helped to serve the midday meal before they sat. They bowed their heads and folded their hands to say grace.

Papá prayed, "Thank you, our Lord, for this food, which we are about to receive from Thy generosity through Christ your son. Amen."

"Amen," everyone said.

Then Papá added, "And we give special thanks today to San Antonio, the saint who helps us find things that we have lost."

"Amen," said everyone again.

"I think today we should thank San Pascual, the

patron saint of cooking, too," said Francisca, when they all began to eat. "These empanadas are perfect."

Antonio piped up. "I helped Carmen and Teresita make them yesterday," he announced proudly.

"Are there enough for me?" someone asked.

They all turned around to see Don Javier.

"Welcome back!" said Papá.

"You must join us," said Tía Dolores. "Please be seated."

Don Javier sat, but Antonio slid out of his own seat and hurried to Don Javier. "Look!" Antonio said with childlike wonder. He held up his carved horse. "One of the three kings brought this red blanket for my horse."

"Did he indeed?" said Don Javier.

Josefina caught his eye, and he winked. Suddenly, Josefina understood. Don Javier had cut off a bit of his own red scarf to make the horse blanket for Antonio! That's why his scarf looked tattered. Someone that nice couldn't possibly be a thief or a trickster who'd taken a ring, could he?

"We missed you, Don Javier," she said shyly. "You seemed worried when you left. I'm glad to see you looking more cheerful."

"I went to Cordero to pay off a debt to a man who lives there," said Don Javier. "Your Tía Dolores can tell you that when she knew me in Mexico City, I was careless and extravagant. I was even more careless than she knew: I lost my estate gambling in a card game. I never told her that the reason I didn't ask her to marry me was that I had no money. Then she left Mexico City, and soon enough, I lost her to a better man, your papá. Truly, I wasn't worthy of her. This past year, I worked hard and earned and saved some money. I came to New Mexico so that I could buy back my estate from the man I'd lost it to. In a few years, my estate will belong to me again. I hope I'll never lose another such treasure as your aunt" (at this, Francisca poked Clara so hard that she yelped) "or my family's legacy. I'll take good care of it."

"I take good care of my horse, don't I?" Antonio piped up.

Grinning, Josefina said, "Sí, Antonio, you're very good at taking care of your horse, and you're good at cooking, too. These empanadas that you made are the best I've ever had! May I have another, please?"

"Sí!" said Antonio, very pleased and proud. Carefully, he chose a particularly big empanada and put it on Josefina's plate. He held her plate aside for a moment before he handed it to her.

"Gracias," said Josefina. She bit into the empanada and *clonk!* "Oh, dear," she murmured. She had not bitten down on pastry and meat, but on something hard. Josefina held up the hard object. "Oh, oh, *oh!*" she exclaimed. *"It's Tía Dolores's ring!"*

"What?"

"The Glowing Heart?"

"My ring?"

"God be praised!"

Everyone exclaimed, loudly and all at once. Then

Josefina gave the ring to Tía Dolores, who asked, "How on earth did my ring end up in an empanada?"

"I did it! I did it!" crowed Antonio.

Suddenly, everyone was silent. They looked at Antonio in disbelief.

Gently, Tía Dolores pulled Antonio onto her lap. "Tell me all about the ring," she said.

Antonio was glad to be the center of attention. He bounced on Tía Dolores's lap. "I took the ring down from the niche by San Pascual," he said, "and I put it in the house of the toy farm. Don Javier said *anything* would be safe in that house."

"I did indeed," said Don Javier.

"So the ring's been in the kitchen all along," groaned Francisca, as if she were at her wits' end. "Antonio hid it in the toy farmhouse."

"Shush," said Josefina. There was no point in being exasperated with the little boy. No one had told him that the ring was precious, or that they feared it had been stolen, or that they'd turned the house upside down looking for it. She urged, "Tell us more, Antonio."

"Everyone liked it when Don Javier and I hid the ring under Tía Dolores's cake on Three Kings' Day," said Antonio, "so I wanted to hide it in a cake again. But you wouldn't let me make another Kings' Cake, Josefina. I waited and waited, and then today I had the idea of squashing the ring into an empanada for someone to find as a surprise." He clapped his hands. "It was a good surprise, wasn't it? You're happy, aren't you?"

"Yes," said Josefina. She leaned forward and hugged Antonio. "We thought the ring was gone. But just like the saint you're named after, San Antonio, you're wonderful at helping us find things that we've lost. So, yes, I am happy." She looked up at Tía Dolores. "I hope that you'll be happy again, too, now that your Glowing Heart ring is back."

"I am *very* happy," said Tía Dolores, "because I'm going to sell the ring so that your Papá won't have to sell his favorite horse, Valiente."

"What?" gasped Francisca, Clara, and Josefina.

"You're going to sell your ring?" asked Josefina. "But we—my sisters and I—well, you've been so tired lately, and so uninterested in food! We thought you were sad and ill because of the *loss* of your Glowing Heart ring."

"Or that you were heartsick because losing the ring reminded you of having lost the life of ease and elegance you had in Mexico City," said Francisca with a romantic sigh and a sideways glance at Don Javier.

"Or that Josefina's cooking had made you ill," Clara added in her no-nonsense way.

Tía Dolores and Papá exchanged a look, and then they both burst out laughing. "No, my dear girls, no," said Tía Dolores. "I love my life here on the rancho with you and your papá. No, the reason I've been tired and uninterested in food is that—God willing—I'm going to have a baby!"

Now *everyone* was laughing and smiling and hugging one another with joy. *Oh!* Josefina was sure that no one had ever been as happy as she was at that moment. She looked at her family, gathered together and blessed with love, and she felt as though surely, surely *her* heart was glowing!

Inside Josefina's World

On a *rancho* like Josefina's, far from the nearest town or neighbor, a visitor's arrival was a special occasion, and guests were welcomed with warmth and generosity. Travelers were always offered a place to sleep for the night, and even a brief visit was celebrated with delicious food served on the family's best dishes.

New Mexicans went to great lengths to welcome guests, but they worked even harder to keep their homes safe from intruders. Outer walls were thick and high. Wooden gates that opened wide to receive visitors and their wagons during the day were barred at night to lock invaders out. Many homes featured tall watchtowers.

Such safeguards were essential because raids by Indians were a regular threat to Spanish settlers. By the time of Josefina's story in the 1820s, the Spanish had long been living in harmony with the Pueblo Indians, but they were in almost constant conflict with the Navajo, Apache, and Comanche. Indian raiders stole horses, sheep, and cattle from Spanish settlements, and Spanish raiders snatched livestock from Indian camps. Both groups kidnapped each other's women and children, who were then sold as slaves or forced to work as servants.

Captives had to learn a new language, answer to a new name, and practice unfamiliar customs. Many were treated inhumanely and never stopped trying to escape.

But some, like Teresita in the story, were not abused and came to accept their new lives. A real-life Navajo *cautiva* named Rosario was offered her freedom after many years as a servant in a Spanish household. Fearing she would no longer know the people in her old home, she chose to stay put. As a gift to her owner, she decided to weave a special *sarape*. "I'll make it a bit Navajo and the rest Spanish," Rosario said, "for I am both now."

Despite their bitter conflict, the Spanish and the Navajo influenced each other in important ways. From the Spanish, Navajo people acquired sheep, which became central to their way of life. They quickly figured out how to breed sheep that were better suited to the harsh climate. Through trade, Spanish farmers then benefited from the sturdier sheep the Navajo had bred.

The two cultures also influenced each other's arts and crafts. Navajo sarapes were prized by settlers for the way their tight weave repelled rain. In turn, Navajo weavers admired a bright red Spanish cloth called *bayeta* and often unraveled it to weave the red threads into their blankets. In this way, the red blankets and thread that appear in this mystery have their own rich story to tell. Just like the sarape Rosario made, they are both Navajo and Spanish—symbols of how traditional ways can be woven together to make something new and beautiful.

GLOSSARY

Spanish Words

Abuelita *(ah-bweh-LEE-tah)*—Grandma

Abuelito *(ah-bweh-LEE-toh)*—Grandpa

adiós *(ah-dee-OHSS)*—good-bye

Albuquerque *(ahl-buh-KEHR-keh)*—a town about sixty miles south of Santa Fe

adobe *(ah-DOH-beh)*—a building material made of earth mixed with straw and water

amigo *(ah-MEE-go)*—friend

Arroyo Blanco (ah-RO-yo BLAHN-ko)—White Arroyo. An *arroyo* is a gully or dry riverbed with steep sides.

Arroyo Verde (ah-RO-yo VEHR-deh)—Green Arroyo

banco *(BAHN-ko)*—a bench built into the wall of a room

bayeta *(bah-YEH-tah)*—a bright red cloth used by Spanish settlers in New Mexico

Bien hecho, mijo! *(bee-en EH-cho mee-jo)*—Well done, my boy!

bizcochito *(beess-ko-CHEE-toh)*—a kind of sugar cookie flavored with anise

buenos días *(BWEH-nohss DEE-ahss)*—good morning

bulto *(BOOL-toh)*—statue

cautiva *(kaw-TEE-vah)*—a female captive. (A male captive is a *cautivo*.)

con permiso *(kohn pehr-MEE-so)*—with your permission

Cordero *(kor-DEH-ro)*—a fictional village. Its name means "Lamb."

curandera *(koo-rahn-DEH-rah)*—a woman who knows how to make medicines from plants and is skilled at healing people

Diablo *(dee-AH-blo)*—the name of a horse that belonged to Don Javier. The word means "Devil."

Don *(DOHN)*—a term of respect for an older man

GLOSSARY

empanada *(em-pah-NAH-dah)*—a small filled pastry, a turnover

excelente *(ehk-seh-LEN-teh)*—excellent

felicidades *(feh-lee-see-DAH-dess)*—congratulations

gracias *(GRAH-see-ahss)*—thank you

Indios *(EEN-dee-ohss)*—Indians; Native Americans

La Fiesta de los Reyes Magos *(lah fee-EHSS-tah deh lohss REH-yess MAH-gohss)*—the Feast of the Three Kings

Lo siento. *(lo see-EN-toh)*—I'm sorry.

Los Cerrillos *(lohss seh-REE-yohss)*—an area south of Santa Fe. Its name means "Small Hills."

mamá *(mah-MAH)*—mother, mama

Muchas gracias. *(MOO-chahss GRAH-see-ahss)*—Thank you very much.

muy bien *(mwee bee-EHN)*—very good

niña *(NEE-nya)*—girl

papá *(pah-PAH)*—father, papa

perdón *(pehr-DOHN)*—pardon

piñón *(pee-NYOHN)*—a kind of short, scrubby pine

por favor *(por fah-VOR)*—please

rancho *(RAHN-cho)*—a farm or ranch

rebozo *(reh-BO-so)*—a kind of long shawl

sala *(SAH-lah)*—a room in a house

San Antonio *(sahn ahn-TOH-nyo)*—Saint Anthony.
Some Catholics believe that Saint Anthony of
Padua can help people find lost or stolen objects.

San Pascual *(sahn pah-SKWAHL)*—Saint Pascual,
the patron saint of cooks

Sangre de Cristo *(SAHN-greh deh KREE-sto)*—a
mountain range in northern New Mexico. Its
name means "Blood of Christ."

Santa Fe *(SAHN-tah FEH)*—the capital city of New
Mexico. Its name means "Holy Faith."

GLOSSARY

sarape *(sah-RAH-peh)*—a warm blanket that is wrapped around the shoulders or worn as a poncho

señor *(seh-NYOR)*—Mr. or sir

señora *(seh-NYO-rah)*—Mrs. or ma'am

señorita *(seh-nyo-REE-tah)*—Miss or young lady

sí *(see)*—yes

Sombrita *(sohm-BREE-tah)*—the name of Josefina's pet goat. The word means "Little Shadow."

tía *(TEE-ah)*—aunt

tortilla *(tor-TEE-yah)*—a kind of flat, round bread

Valiente *(vah-lee-EN-teh)*—brave, valiant

vamos *(VAH-mohss)*—let's go

Vaya con Dios. *(VAH-yah kohn dee-OHSS)*—Farewell. The literal meaning of the words is "Go with God."

y *(ee)*—and

Yo te prometo. *(yo teh pro-MEH-toh)*—I promise you.

Read more of JOSEFINA'S stories,

available from booksellers and at *americangirl.com*

❧ *Classics* ☙

Josefina's classic series, now in two volumes:

Volume 1:
Sunlight and Shadows
Josefina and her sisters are excited when Tía Dolores comes to their *rancho*, bringing new ideas, new fashions, and new challenges. Can Josefina open her heart to change and still hold on to precious memories of Mamá?

Volume 2:
Second Chances
Josefina makes a wonderful discovery: She has a gift for healing. Can she find the courage and creativity to mend her family's broken trust in an *americano* trader and keep her family whole and happy when Tía Dolores plans to leave?

❧ *Journey in Time* ☙

Travel back in time—and spend a day with Josefina!

Song of the Mockingbird
Spend a cozy evening at the *rancho*, come face-to-face with a snarling mountain lion, or visit the lively market in Santa Fe. Choose your own path through this multiple-ending story!

❧ *Mystery* ☙

Suspense and sleuthing with Josefina!

Secrets in the Hills
Josefina has heard tales of treasure buried in the hills, and of a ghostly Weeping Woman who roams at night. But she never imagined the stories might be true—until a mysterious stranger arrives at her *rancho*.

A Sneak Peek at

Secrets
in the Hills

A Josefina Mystery

Step into another suspenseful
adventure with Josefina!

TÍA DOLORES KEPT Josefina, Francisca, and Clara busy for the rest of the day. The girls helped the servants dig beets from the garden and lug the year's first pumpkins into the kitchen to be sliced and dried.

When the afternoon shadows had lengthened across the courtyard, Francisca stopped and stretched. "I'll make the *tortillas* for the evening meal," she offered. "That job will give me a rest!"

Josefina eased a pumpkin to the floor. "And I'll bring water from the stream," she offered. She fetched the water jar and headed through the courtyard.

As she stepped outside, she squinted into the late afternoon sun. Someone was riding on horseback toward the rancho. No, two people.

Josefina darted back inside. In recent years, there had been many incidents of bandits and raiders causing trouble in New Mexico.

She found her *papá* with a servant, Miguel, inspecting a harness that needed repair. "Papá!" she called breathlessly. "Two riders are approaching the rancho. I don't recognize them."

"Wait inside," Papá instructed calmly, dusting his hands on his trousers. "I'll meet our visitors. Miguel, come with me."

By the time the strangers neared the rancho, Josefina, Francisca, and Clara were pressed near the high, barred window in the front storeroom, which overlooked the road. "Come away, girls," Tía Dolores called from the kitchen. "It's impolite to stare like frightened prairie dogs."

Francisca dared a last peek out the window. "One of the men is slumped over, as if he's sick or hurt," she whispered. "I think the other one is an *americano*."

An americano! Josefina exchanged a surprised glance with Clara. They had met a number of americanos—English-speaking men who brought caravans of covered wagons full of trade goods from the United States. Papá had done business with them. But Josefina had seen americanos only in Santa Fe.

"Dolores!" Papá's shout drifted through the window. "We need your help."

Josefina and her sisters followed Tía Dolores toward the front gate just as Miguel led the two horses into the courtyard. The americano, who looked no older than Josefina's sister Ana, dismounted and helped Papá ease the second man from his saddle. "Gracias," the americano said in badly accented Spanish. His hair was the color of ripe wheat. Hours spent outdoors had tanned his skin.

The injured man's hair was black, his skin the color of tea. His trousers and *sarape* looked as dusty as a field worker's after a hard day of harvest. His boots looked hard-used as well, although he seemed unable to put much weight on his left leg. A blood-stained bandage, perhaps made from his shirt, was tied just below the knee. "My name is Pedro Zamora," he gasped in a voice tight with pain. "I am a *rastreador*, seeking a chestnut mare. Her owner does not know if the horse is lost or was stolen. I—"

"Por favor, take him into the spare sleeping *sala*," Tía Dolores interrupted, putting aside the polite introductions. Señor Zamora's eyes closed, and he would have slumped to the ground if the americano and Papá hadn't supported him.

Tía Dolores shooed the men forward with a wave of her hand. "Francisca and Clara," she said over her shoulder, "go back to the kitchen and help finish our meal. Josefina, come with me."

Josefina's stomach made a fist. *Oh, Tía Magdalena,* she thought. *I wish you were here to treat his wounds.*

"Wait here a moment," Tía Dolores instructed Josefina when they reached the doorway of the sala. Then she followed the americano and Papá as they helped Señor Zamora inside.

Josefina tried to imagine how the stranger might have injured himself. He was a rastreador—a tracker. Rancho owners sometimes hired trackers if valuable horses or cattle went missing. Why was he traveling with an americano?

A few moments later Tía Dolores reappeared. "Señor Zamora cut his leg," she told Josefina. "The wound is beginning to fester, and he has a fever."

Josefina stared at Señor Zamora, who was tucked into bed like a child. His forehead glistened with sweat, and he was mumbling under his breath. "What is he saying?"

Tía Dolores shook her head. "He's not making sense. That can happen with high fevers. Will you fetch more water, please? I'll have his leg bandaged by the time you return."

Josefina saw Señor Zamora's face in her mind as she hurried to the stream with a water jar. Had the mysterious stranger been sent to test her healing skills and knowledge?

As Josefina returned to the sala, she heard Tía Dolores talking to Señor Zamora in a soothing tone. "Your things are safe here, señor."

"Is his mind clearer?" Josefina asked, putting the water jar by the bed.

Tía Dolores shook her head. "Not really. He seems to be worried about his clothes." She gestured to a pile by the door. "Miguel provided our guest with a clean shirt to wear."

"We should put a damp cloth on his forehead," Josefina said. "That will help bring his fever down."

"You go ahead," Tía Dolores said. "I need to make sure that dinner preparations are well in hand. I'll return in a moment."

Josefina poured water into a bowl, wrung out a cloth, folded it neatly, and draped it over her patient's forehead. His eyes opened for a moment, as if he was startled by the coolness. "Señorita?" he whispered.

"My name is Josefina."

Señor Zamora clutched her arm with unexpected strength. "Por favor—where is my sarape?"

"Right over there." Josefina waved her hand toward the pile of clothes. "Don't worry, señor. With God's help, you will soon be well."

His hand fell back to the blanket, and his eyes

flickered closed. Josefina touched the damp cloth and found it already warm. She replaced the cloth with another, and Señor Zamora began to murmur again. "The search . . . I must continue my search . . ."

"No, señor," Josefina told him quietly. "Your search for the horse can wait."

His head turned from side to side. "The rock," he muttered. "I found the rock."

Josefina bit her lip. "Please, señor," she begged. "Try to rest."

Teresita entered the sala, her quiet calm as comforting as Tía Dolores's brisk efficiency. "Your aunt asked me to sit with him," she told Josefina. "How is he?"

"Not well," Josefina said, regarding their visitor.

Teresita gave Josefina a reassuring smile. "Don't worry, Señorita Josefina. If God wills it, our guest will recover."

Josefina nodded. She'd done what she could for Señor Zamora.

As she left the sala, she carried his dirty sarape
out to the courtyard. It was too late in the day to
launder his filthy shirt and trousers, but she could at
least shake the dust from his sarape. It had once been
of good quality, woven well of yellow and blue and
red wool, but Josefina had trouble seeing the pattern
through the dirt.

She gripped the woven cloak by the edge and
gave it a hard, snapping shake. A cloud of dust
billowed into the air. And something white fluttered
to the ground.

Josefina stooped to pick up the piece of paper.
It was thin, stained, and tattered. Three sides of the
paper were cut straight. The fourth was ragged, as if
this piece had come from a larger piece of paper that
had been torn in two.

Squinting at the faded ink, Josefina made out an
outline that looked familiar: a tall column supporting a flat surface. *That looks like Balancing Rock!* she
thought. Was *that* the rock Señor Zamora had been

speaking of? She tried to make out the other faint sketches: arrows, a turtle, curved lines that looked like a rainbow—

A burst of conversation from the kitchen interrupted Josefina's study, and her cheeks grew warm. This paper didn't belong to her! Taking a closer look at Señor Zamora's sarape, she found that he had stitched a small piece of thin hide to the inside of the cloak, making a hidden pocket. The map must have fallen from that pocket when she shook the sarape.

Clara appeared at the kitchen door. "Josefina? We're ready for the evening meal."

"Coming!" Josefina called. She slipped the fragile map carefully back into the sarape's hidden pocket, gently brushed what dust she could from the cloak, and folded it in such a way that the pocket—and the map it contained—lay flat. Then she returned the sarape to the sala. Whenever Señor Zamora was ready to be on his way, he would find his map just where he had left it.

But tucking the map away couldn't erase it from Josefina's mind. She remembered Miguel's reaction when they had found a cross scratched into the wall of a cave only a few days before: "If God wants me to find buried treasure, I hope He will send me a map!"

Señor Zamora had told Miguel that he'd been searching for a missing mare. Yet his map, old as it was, had surely not been drawn to show him where to look for a horse! He was searching for something else, she was sure of it. Something secret. So . . . what was he seeking?

About the Author

VALERIE TRIPP says that she became
a writer because of the kind of person she is.
She says she's curious, and writing requires
you to be interested in everything. Talking
is her favorite sport, and writing is a way of
talking on paper. She's a daydreamer, which
helps her come up with her ideas. And she
loves words. She even loves the struggle
to come up with just the right words as
she writes and rewrites. Ms. Tripp lives in
Maryland with her husband.